'Goodnight, Mr Sanguardo,' Celeste said, her smile flickering uncertainly.

For a moment she just went on standing there, looking at him.

Letting the impact he made on her retinas be absorbed into her.

'Goodnight, Celeste,' Rafael answered. He gave her a brief nod of farewell and got back into the car. The chauffeur slammed the door and went to the driver's seat.

Celeste stepped inside the entrance hall, shut the door and went upstairs. Her heart-rate was raised, she knew.

It's the stairs—just the stairs—because I'm hurrying too much!

But it was not the stairs. For as she turned on the light in her flat and went to the living room windows to pull the curtains, and looked down to the pavement at the car starting to pull into the road now that she was safely inside, she could feel her heart's hectic beating.

And she knew exactly what had caused it.

Rafael Sanguardo…

His name echoed in her head. Circling around. Not letting her go.

Julia James lives in England with her family. Harlequin Mills & Boon® were the first 'grown-up' books she read as a teenager, alongside Georgette Heyer and Daphne du Maurier, and she's been reading them ever since. Julia adores the English and Celtic countryside, in all its seasons, and is fascinated by all things historical, from castles to cottages. She also has a special love for the Mediterranean—'The most perfect landscape after England!'—and considers both ideal settings for romance stories. In between writing she enjoys walking, gardening, needlework, baking extremely gooey cakes and trying to stay fit!

Recent titles by the same author:

PAINTED THE OTHER WOMAN
THE DARK SIDE OF DESIRE
FROM DIRT TO DIAMONDS
FORBIDDEN OR FOR BEDDING?

**Did you know these are also available as eBooks?
Visit www.millsandboon.co.uk**

THE
FORBIDDEN TOUCH
OF SANGUARDO

BY
JULIA JAMES

MILLS
BOON

Published in Great Britain 2014
by Mills & Boon, an imprint of Harlequin (UK) Limited,
Eton House, 18-24 Paradise Road, Richmond, Surrey, TW9 1SR

© 2014 Julia James

ISBN: 978 0 263 24217 1

THE
FORBIDDEN TOUCH
OF SANGUARDO

To the utterly unforgettable holidays I've been privileged to have in Hawaii, which inspired the romantic setting for Celeste and Rafael. (And, yes, I did go on a star-gazing expedition—just like they did!!!!)

CHAPTER ONE

CELESTE STOOD POISED at the head of the long curving flight of marble stairs that led down into the great hall below. It was already crowded with people in black tie and evening clothes, and servers were circulating with trays of champagne and canapés. Her fellow models for the evening were mingling in evening dress, prior to the charity fashion show that was about to start. She had arrived slightly late at the stately home in Oxfordshire that was the evening's venue, but had seized the last-minute opportunity to be here tonight, well away from London—and from Karl Reiner.

Celeste's expression tautened even just from her thinking about the man. She had known when she became the new face of Blonde Visage, one of the skincare ranges belonging to Reiner Visage—one for each complexion type—that Karl Reiner liked to have a more than professional relationship with the Reiner Visage models, but because he had been preoccupied with another 'face'—Monique Silva—Celeste had felt it safe to allow herself to be tempted by the lucrative contract. Making good, regular money was, even after years in the fickle and intensely competitive modelling business, not something to turn down lightly.

A bleak expression lit the back of her eyes.

There was never, *ever,* any such thing as easy money— She of all people should know that…

For now Karl had tired of Monique and was turning his

attention to Celeste—and he assumed she would be as willing as Monique had been.

Celeste's expression hardened. Karl Reiner could assume what he liked, but he would not get what he was after from her. Not even now he had flown in from New York this weekend specifically to pressure her to extend her contract—and pay the price he wanted her to pay for it.

Well, she would not be extending it. Yes, the money had been good, but these days making money was not the be all and end all of her preoccupations. A cold miasma seemed to touch at her skin. Not any more...

Her refusal was a message Karl Reiner didn't want to hear, and he had demanded she make herself available to have dinner with him in London tonight. To evade him Celeste had been obliged to volunteer at a late hour for the charity fashion show that was shortly to take place in the grand salon.

Just thinking about Karl Reiner and what he wanted of her—what he thought she would provide—intensified the feeling of a cold miasma on her skin. It was penetrating into her like a toxic memory, fetid and foul...

With effort, she pushed it from her mind.

No! She would not think—would not remember.

She had dealt with those memories long ago! Paid the price for dealing with them—a price she was still paying, must always pay—and it was a price she paid because there was no alternative. Could never be.

All she could do was what she had done for years now—build her career, focus only on that. Be dedicated, hard-working.

On her own.

Always on her own.

For a last fleeting moment the bleakness showed in her eyes again. She knew far too well the price she was paying for those memories whose dank tendrils dragged across her flesh.

A stab of self-revulsion jabbed at her. Once she had lacerated herself with such stabs, but she gave herself a mental shake. She would not let anything drag her mind down such dark pathways. She was here tonight to do a job. One she had done a hundred times before.

Yet as she gathered her long skirts gracefully, preparing to descend into the thronged hall below, something stayed her for one last moment. She felt as if something *were* different tonight. As if she were poised on the edge of her familiar world. On the threshold of a new one.

Then, with a sharp, dismissive intake of breath, she took a step forward and started to move down the staircase. There was no new world awaiting her. There could not be.

She did not need the echo of that trailing miasma across her skin to tell her that...

Rafael Sanguardo stood, empty champagne glass loosely held in long fingers, and let his dark gaze rest on his opulently baroque surroundings, painted and gilded to profusion. It was an irony not lost on him that, as one of the sponsors of the charity, he should be a guest here—considering that it had been the exploited wealth of the Americas that had built this eighteenth-century splendour and that it had been the labour of his *peon* ancestors, albeit under Spanish colonial masters and not British ones, who had so signally contributed to this display of old-world wealth.

But now history had turned its wheel of fortune. In the global village of the twenty-first century it was the industrious entrepreneurship of former colonials who generated much of the world's wealth—and Rafael Sanguardo knew he could count himself one of their number.

Thanks to his own intelligence, determination and drive, he had transformed himself in little more than a dozen years from an orphaned teenager living in one of the smallest of the string of countries stretching from Mexico to Colombia, via a philanthropic scholarship to a prestigious North American university, into a serial entrepreneur who had backed a succession of highly successful companies and who could now, had he so wished, have made his home in just such a palatial pile as the one he was tonight a guest in.

That was not his preference, however. He was footloose, preferring to rent apartments in London and New York and stay in hotels in whichever other countries he did business in. 'Settling down' was not on his agenda.

Not any more.

Madeline had seen to that.

Into his head stabbed the last words she had thrown at him. Mocking. Furious. Thwarted.

'Why, Rafe, darling, what a puritan you are!'

But her taunting had masked anger, lashing out at him. Repelling him as much as what she had disclosed to him had repelled him.

Repelled him still…

He pulled his thoughts away. Madeline was history. Out of his life. And she should be out of his head, too. She was not worth even the memory…

There was only one thing Madeline was worth—had only ever been worth—and that was what was most precious to her.

Money.

Rafael's mouth tightened. His eyes darkened. Well, now Madeline had all the money she craved—but money was all she had. Even though she had once craved more. Memory darkened his expression again. She had once craved *him*— craved everything that had once been between them.

Their affair had lit up like a torch between them. It had been a match that had seemed to be ideally cast. He the self-made, darkly handsome Latino multimillionaire, she the British flame-haired British beauty whose business abilities had made her as rich as him. They had been a wealthy, glamorous couple, cutting a swathe wherever they went.

Then it had ended.

Like an unwelcome replay, he saw the scene inside his head yet again.

Madeline was looking at him. Looking at him with her almond-shaped emerald eyes from where she lay on the bed, her fabulous auburn hair tumbling sensuously around her naked shoulders. Her lush, peaked breasts were on show for him. So was the rest of her curved, enticing body. She lay, lounging back on the pillows. Alluring. Seductive.

'Now tell me you don't want me, Rafe, darling,' she purred.

She let her thighs slacken, easing her hand sensually along the divide between her legs.

He walked to the bedroom door. Turned to look at her. Still repelled.

'Be gone by the time I get back,' he told her.

Then he left.

He heard her laughter—that rich, mocking laughter—infused with what he knew was a jibing anger at him for his rejection of her, following him as he shut the front door of his apartment behind him.

It tried to follow him still, that mocking, jibing, angry laughter, as he knew she wanted it to.

But its power was gone.

Just as Madeline had gone. Out of his life—totally.

Now even the thought of Madeline repelled him. As did everything about her...her looks, her attitude, her ambition, her values. *Everything.*

A hovering waiter pulled him back to where he was, and with a slight smile of thanks Rafael placed his glass on the extended tray. As he turned back, something caught his eye.

Some*one.*

Walking down the sweeping staircase with an aura about her that made his gaze focus piercingly. Taking in everything about her.

Pale beauty. Hair caught in a chignon the colour of champagne at the nape of her swan-like neck. Her face was in profile. Perfect profile. As perfect as her tall, slender body, sheathed in a single-shouldered ecru gown that moulded slight breasts, draped slender hips and dropped down long, long legs to skim slim ankles, revealed by the draping of her skirts, around which snaked the clasp of her heeled evening shoes.

She must surely be one of the models, he realised. Her height, her slenderness, the way she held herself, the way she wore her clearly couture gown—all indicated that. As she reached the foot of the stairs she blended into the throng and was lost to his view. He craned his head a moment, seeking her, but could not see her.

A sense of frustration at her disappearance caught at him. Then he stilled, frowning for a quite different reason. A jolt of realisation.

This was the first woman who had caught his attention since he had severed all links with Madeline—

Oh, plenty of women had sought his attention—he was well used to that—but in the grim aftermath of Madeline none had been of any interest to him.

So what is it about this one?

Yet even as the question formed he knew it was redundant. He could answer it immediately.

She is nothing at all like Madeline!

Madeline's richly hued flashy beauty and her egoistic temperament had demanded that everyone look at her. The pale girl descending the staircase had looked as cool as Madeline had been fiery.

But there was more to the difference than looks, he sensed. Madeline would have descended the grand staircase like a drama queen, wanting everyone to gaze at her. To admire and envy her. To desire her.

This pale blonde girl had slipped down the steps as quietly as a ghost—as if she were not quite part of this world, as if she wanted no eyes drawn to her. Odd, he mused, in someone who was a model. If, of course, she *was* one.

Well, he thought, impatient to see her again, if she were, he had better go and take his seat and find out.

One thing he knew with certainty: whoever the pale, elusive blonde was, he wanted to see her again. His dark eyes glinted. Finally he'd seen a woman to spark his interest—an interest he definitely wanted to pursue. Would that interest survive acquaintance with her? Or would getting to know her put him off, despite that incredible pale beauty of hers?

Will she prove as flawed as Madeline?

That was the question that haunted him.

CHAPTER TWO

THE MUSIC WAS starting up—glitteringly baroque Vivaldi to suit the era of the house—and in well-practised order the models issued out onto the runway constructed down the centre of the long salon.

The first gown was the same one the models had worn while mingling with the guests, and Celeste was glad of it. It was exactly the kind of gown she would have chosen for herself, had she been a guest. Flattering, but revealing nothing more than a bare shoulder, and in one of the pale colours that she liked. Another model had once told her she must like disappearing into the background. Celeste had only smiled slightly. But the girl had been right, for all that.

Muted, understated, discreet—those were the fashion watchwords she adhered to. And one more, too.

Modest.

Not for her, in her own clothes, plunging necklines or thigh-skimming hemlines. Even on the beach she preferred a one-piece.

Now, as she swished along the runway, she felt the tension that had assailed her as she'd stood at the top of the stairs evaporate. Years of experience as a model made this kind of tightly choreographed display second nature to her, and she walked with assurance and poise until, at the foot of the runway, she paused to reverse her direction.

And froze.

Dark, long-lashed eyes, focussed on her. A shadowed face with lean cheeks, incised features. A mouth with deep lines around it. A sculpted jawline. Night-dark hair.

For a timeless moment the impression carved itself into her vision. Then, with a jolt, she knew she must start walking again. Jerkily, she paced back up to the head of the runway and was swept offstage into the melee of the changing area, to emerge minutes later in a vivid scarlet evening gown. All the way down the runway she was conscious of the man sitting at the far end. Wondering whether he'd be watching her.

Hectically, her thoughts tumbled inside her head. She'd been eyed up often enough in her time as a model—and even though she didn't like it she never let it affect her.

So why had this man's regard so affected her? Why had it impacted on her in the few seconds she'd had to register it? What was so different about it? About him…?

As she neared the end of the runway she steeled herself for that dark, penetrating gaze—which didn't come. As she glanced briefly in his direction she saw that his attention was on his mobile phone. He was tapping in a text, long legs extended, completely ignoring her.

Immediately she felt her tension drop. She turned, skilfully manoeuvring her skirts, and plunged back up the runway. *So much for that!* she thought, with a wry dart of self-mockery.

Had she turned her head again, however, she might have felt differently.

Rafael's eyes had lifted from his phone and were settled, instead, on her retreating form. They went on watching until she disappeared. Then, and only then, did he resume his tapping.

He found, however, that his mind was not on his emails.

The show was over, the applause was dying away and guests were heading off for the buffet supper awaiting them in the dining room across the entrance hall.

Rafael got to his feet. There was a sense of purpose about him. The models would be mingling with the guests again and he wanted to find her—stake his claim before anyone else could be as drawn to her pale, haunting beauty as he was.

But as his eyes searched the crowded dining room it came to him that she simply was not there. The other models were—but not the one he wanted to see. He frowned. So where was she? He crossed the hallway back into the salon, where the runway was being dismantled by workmen. Still no sign of her.

He saw that a glass door to the side was open, and slipped through on impulse. He found himself out on a terrace and walked down it to the end. Turning the corner, he saw gardens stretching out before him. Steps swept down to the level of the lawns.

A figure had paused at the edge. A female figure, her evening gown pale in the dim light, craning her neck upwards. But she wasn't looking back at the mansion. She was looking up at the night sky.

Rafael's dark eyes glinted in the starlight and he started to walk down the steps towards her.

Celeste was gazing upwards, rapt. It was a glorious starry night! In London stars were, at best, dim and hazy. But here in the countryside they were bright and vivid, the mighty sweep of the Milky Way clear in the heavens. So unimaginably distant…

Once she had wanted only to be taken up amongst them, leaving the earth far, far behind…

'The ancient Chinese believed that the Milky Way was the source of the Yellow River.'

The voice came from behind her.

Celeste swirled round. There was little light, but she did not need light to tell her who this was. It was the man who had been looking at her as she'd walked along the runway.

The man who had made her aware of him as no man ever had…

He was heading towards her. She could not see his features, only his height, his strolling elegance as he came to stand beside her. She heard the deep, accented timbre of his voice as he spoke again. Felt her nerve-endings start to send messages to her she did *not* want to feel!

'They have a legend,' he went on, 'that says two lovers were cruelly parted by their parents and placed on either side of the Milky Way—the galactic river. We see them as stars, forever gazing at each other.'

He was looking at her as he spoke. Taking in her frozen stance, the sudden tension in her face. She looked, he thought, as if she was going to bolt—a reaction he found unusual in a woman. Long experience had taught him that women welcomed his attentions.

Madeline certainly had.

But she is not Madeline.

And that was what he wanted, he reminded himself. For her to be utterly different. So it was good that she was reacting as she was, wasn't it? But whatever the reason for her radiating wariness on all frequencies he wanted to dispel it.

'It's incredible, isn't it?' he said, keeping his tone conversational. 'To think of the vast distances of the heavens. Our galaxy is just one of billions, each with billions of stars.' He frowned slightly. 'Some of the stars we think of as stars are galaxies themselves. Andromeda is our closest, and it is…' He searched the sky with his eyes.

'It's there,' Celeste heard herself saying. 'In the Andromeda constellation, between Pegasus and Cassiopeia. The galaxy is M31—Messier body thirty-one—but it's not actually the closest galaxy to us, only to the Milky Way overall. It's going to merge with the Milky Way eventually, and form a giant elliptical galaxy in a few billion years.'

She pointed jerkily upwards, mentally castigating herself

for gabbling about galaxies and constellations, but other than marching away it had seemed the safest thing to do.

Though 'safe' was the very last thing she felt...

Her nerve-endings were firing in a way that she had never before experienced.

Rafael followed her gaze, then glanced across at her. Wanting to look at her. Wanting her to look at him. Wanting her to speak again.

He smiled appreciatively. 'You're very knowledgeable,' he remarked.

'I like stars,' she answered, in the same abrupt, jerky manner. 'They're very far away.'

Even as she spoke she started. *Why did I say that? Why am I standing here talking to him—letting him talk to me?*

And why was the deep, accented timbre of his voice reaching into her? Disturbing her...firing all her nerves at high pitch...

'Is that a commendation?' he asked dryly.

'Yes,' she answered.

As if she'd realised it was a strange thing to say, he saw her give a tiny shake of her head. As she did so, he saw her change. She dipped her head, tightened her grip on her skirts. Getting a grip, belatedly, on the situation. A situation she was going to terminate right now. Because she did not let situations like this arise.

But there's never been a situation like this...no man has ever made me react like this!

Which made it all the more imperative that she get away from him—right now! Stop this before it started.

'Excuse me,' she said. 'I must go back inside.'

Her voice had changed, too. It was clipped now, and quite impersonal.

Distant.

'Permit me to escort you.' Rafael's voice was smooth.

She did not hesitate. 'Thank you—no.'

Her tone was decisive, and before his eyes she turned and walked back up the steps. He looked after her.

From chatting about stars to cutting him dead—all in under a minute.

No, nothing like Madeline at all...

Celeste gained the salon and walked rapidly across it. Her heart-rate was up, and it was not because of her rapid ascent of the exterior steps. What on earth had she just gone and done? Standing there with that man, talking about astronomy! She'd gone out to the gardens for two reasons— to take advantage of the clear night sky and to delay having to mix socially. Because over supper she would inevitably see that man again.

The man who had come in search of her.

Because of course that was what he'd been doing! She wasn't an idiot—no one struck up a conversation about galaxies with a lone female if they weren't trying to chat her up! Then, to make her heart-rate race even more, a mortifying thought struck her. Had he thought she was standing out there stargazing in order to deliberately invite him to talk to her?

She felt her cheeks flush. Well, it didn't matter. It didn't matter either way. Because from now on she was going to avoid him totally until she could decently get away back to Oxford and the hotel room she'd booked. Staying well out of London and away from Karl Reiner for as long as possible.

But she didn't want to think about the repulsive Karl Reiner. And she didn't want to think about the man who had set her nerve-endings firing, elevated her heart-rate. A man who did not repel her.

Who attracted her—

No! A little twist of bitterness clenched inside her. What did it matter if, however inexplicably, he attracted her? It didn't matter! It *couldn't* matter.

It could never matter...

A dull, familiar stab jabbed at her.

I am what my past has made me and nothing can change that—nothing!

And men—all men—could be nothing of her present now.

Face set, she gained the dining room, forcing herself to take a breath—to assume the appearance, if nothing else, of calm. She made her way to one of the buffet tables around the edge, glad to see Zoe, a fellow model, there. They helped themselves to some undressed salad and a slice of chicken each.

'So,' said Zoe invitingly as they started to eat their meagre portions, 'what are you going to do about the guy who couldn't take his eyes off you? Has he made a move on you already?'

Celeste tensed. 'No,' she lied, trying to sound nonchalant.

'Shame,' said the other girl. '*I'd* go for him. Looks *and* dosh! Rafael Sanguardo. South American. He's a zillionaire investor. Used to hang out with that glitzy redhead on the *Top Ten Rich Women* list—Madeline Walters. Hotshot and hot totty! She made a fortune for herself and headed for the States to make another pile of dough. Of course...' she threw a sly glance at Celeste '...*you've* got Karl Reiner panting around after you, haven't you? Now he's through with Monique Silva. Mind you,' she added, 'I know which man *I'd* rather have in bed beside me! Señor Tall, Dark and *Very* Handsome Sanguardo! Creepy Karl wouldn't get a look-in!' She drew breath. 'Well, I'd better network. Plenty of useful contacts out there—and loads of loaded guys! And standing here by all this food is torture. See you!'

She sauntered off, leaving Celeste to her supper and her thoughts.

Rafael Sanguardo...

The name glided through her head. She'd never heard of him, but from the way Zoe had talked about him it sounded as if he was on the 'Mr Available and Rich' list that a lot of models made it their business to know about. She speared a sliver of chicken with decided resolve. Rafael Sanguardo was none of *her* business, and he would stay that way.

'May I help you to something more from the buffet?'

The deep, faintly accented voice addressing her was familiar.

And very unwelcome.

She turned. It was Rafael Sanguardo.

Celeste felt herself tense automatically. But not just because he was the one person here she wanted to avoid. For the first time she was seeing him in full light, rather than dim glimpses. And everything she'd glimpsed about him was overwhelmingly reinforced. He was, just as Zoe had flippantly called him, Mr Tall, Dark and *Very* Handsome! But it was not smooth, playboy-style looks that he possessed. His face was lean, with a tough-looking jawline, high cheekbones and a strong nose. But it wasn't those features that held her. It was the eyes.

They were dark—incredibly dark—with a hawkish look to them, and they were resting on her with an expression in them that instantly made her breathless.

How? How is this happening? she thought with a hollowing of her stomach. It *never* happened! Men could look her over and she'd be immune to it! Immune the way she *had* to be. But this man—*somehow*—was having this extraordinary effect on her, and she didn't know why.

All she knew, with a surge of intense self-preserving urgency, was that she had to stop it happening. Had to stop looking at him—stop looking at the way his long, lean body, darkly clad in what she knew must be a hand-tailored tuxedo, easily topped six feet, the way his DJ moulded his shoulders. His gleaming white dress shirt performed the same office for his torso, telling her that his physique was as honed as the planes of his face.

He was addressing her again, in that deep, accented voice that did things to her she did not want it to do! What had he just said? She had to reply—say something, anything—then walk away! *Food—he asked you about food! Do you want any? That was it.*

With effort, she found a brief reply. 'Thank you, but this is enough,' she managed to say.

An eyebrow quirked over the incredibly dark eyes that looked as if they were hewn from some ancient, volcanic rock. *Basalt,* she thought, *or obsidian...darker than slate.*

'It doesn't look enough for a sparrow,' he murmured. The dark eyes glanced at her. 'Fortunately you don't appear to have the starved, size-zero look about you that so many models have.'

Celeste could hear condemnation of excessive thinness in his voice. 'Models *have* to be thin!' she was stung into retorting. She was not objecting to his criticism of size-zero models, but to the way his eyes had washed over her. The effect that slow wash had had on her...

'It's shamefully perverse for women in the developed world to ape those who go hungry from necessity, not fashion!' he returned sharply.

She took a breath, making herself answer honestly. 'You are right,' she admitted.

For a moment she let her eyes meet his in acknowledgement of the truth of what he had just said. It was a mistake. For one endless moment she had the strangest sensation that she was drowning—drowning in a deep, fathomless ocean. Then, with an effort, she pulled her gaze away. Found that she was trembling with the effort.

'I'm sorry—that was very blunt of me,' she heard him respond. 'Though it is a pity that you will not try some of these richer foods.' He indicated the lavish spread in front of them.

Celeste glanced at them, and then back at the man who was so disturbing her. 'They do look delicious,' she allowed. 'But I mustn't.'

'You won't be tempted?' he said.

There was a trace of humour now in his accented voice. A trace that did yet more disturbing things to her. As did the glint in his eyes that told her it was more than food he wanted her to be tempted by.

She gave a decisive shake of her head. Time to stop this— right now.

'No,' she replied. Her voice was polite, but firm. She put down her now empty plate. Looked back at him. Made herself look at him but not react to him. Made herself say in a polite, social voice, using just the sort of tone she might use to anyone at all, 'Do please excuse me, but I have to circulate and show off this dress.'

She gave a smile—brief, polite, perfunctory. But this time she did not meet his eyes. Instead, she turned away, tall and graceful, and threaded her way into the throng.

Behind her, Rafael watched her disappear. Her second disappearing act of the evening.

Why? Why does she run from me?

That was the question uppermost in his mind—except for his overwhelming consciousness that in this second all too brief encounter his interest in her had not diminished, but intensified.

There is something about her that is drawing me to her— something powerful, irresistible, overwhelming.

Something that was sending a pulse through him. Something that was engendered by that extraordinary pale, pure beauty she possessed—the turn of her head, the flawless translucence of her alabaster skin, the perfect features of her face, delicate and exquisitely cut, the clear, luminous grey-blue of her eyes.

He knew with absolute certainty that he had felt something when she had turned that gaze on him, fully meeting his own—it was a gaze whose very brevity had told him that whatever the cause of her insistence on walking away from him, which she had now exhibited twice—it was not because she was irresponsive to him.

It is the same for her as it is for me! I know it. The stillness, the betraying dilation of her pupils, the sudden intake of breath, the collision of her eyes with mine—acknowledges, confirms her reaction to me—

It had told him all he needed to know…

Whatever had made her walk away, it was not because she was immune to him. So why had she? An unwelcome explanation intruded. Was it because she was already involved elsewhere? A burning urge to find out consumed him. Yet he did not even know her name.

He inhaled sharply, pulling himself together. It would be easy enough to find out everything he needed to know about her. She was a model, she worked for an agency, and that meant the information was out there. And if the answer was the one he realised he wanted it to be more with every passing moment, then he would set out to woo her—woo her and win her.

His imagination raced ahead, vivid and eager.

In his mind's eye he saw himself gazing into her eyes, clasping her hand, drawing her towards him, taking her slender, pliant body into his arms and lowering his mouth to her tremulous, tender lips, tasting their sweetness, seeking the nectar within, feeling her respond to his embrace, her body contouring against his with soft sensuousness, glowing with honeyed desire as her breasts peaked against him…

But imagination was not enough! He wanted the reality.

The reality of her pale, pure beauty, which was calling to him with a subtly compelling, insistent power that was impossible to deny.

CHAPTER THREE

'YOU WANT MORE money to renew your contract. That's it, isn't it?' Karl Reiner's voice grated.

Celeste kept her expression fixed. Karl Reiner had demanded her presence at a dinner in a West End hotel hosted by a fashion magazine keen on retaining its share of the lavish Reiner Visage advertising budget. Since she was still—just—under contract, it had been impossible for her to decline.

She deeply wished she had. Wished she could just walk off the way she had when Rafael Sanguardo had made a move on her at the charity event the previous weekend.

Not, she found herself thinking, that anyone in their right mind would put Karl Reiner and Rafael Sanguardo in the same class. The difference was total. Karl's stocky stature and slack belly were the complete opposite of Rafael Sanguardo's tall, lean, honed physique—just as Karl's pouched, close-set eyes were a million miles from the dark, hawkish eyes that had rested so disturbingly on her. And Karl's receding dyed hair, swept back into a ponytail that he mistakenly seemed to think made him look creative and bohemian, had nothing of the feathered sable of the South American's.

Yet again Celeste felt the disquieting quickening of her pulse as an image of Rafael Sanguardo took shape in her mind. It had been doing so repeatedly ever since the weekend. She had tried desperately hard to put him out of her mind but it had been impossible—just impossible! She could bewail it all she liked, try as hard as she could, but it was no good. That encounter, however brief, had imprinted itself on her. Why, she did not know—could not understand. Could not understand why her habitual immunity to men was failing her so pitiably when it came to Rafael Sanguardo.

But if she couldn't understand it at least she could do her determined best to ignore it. Suppress it and crush it out of her consciousness—out of her life. There was no point— none whatsoever!—in thinking about him.

What Rafael Sanguardo wanted was not what she was free to want…

An old, familiar ripple of revulsion went through her. Those slimy trails across her skin—fetid memory made tangible.

And with Karl Reiner pressingly at her side tonight, making her skin crawl, revulsion came afresh. Recrimination came in its wake. Why, oh, why had she ever got involved with Reiner Visage?

But she knew the reason now—just as she had long ago. Rejection seared within her.

This is different! Entirely different! Karl Reiner can assume what he likes. I will never go along with it!

Nor was there anything he could say that would make her sign a new contract. She would simply go on stonewalling him, staying as composed and as civil as she could, until she was free in a few weeks' time.

But his persistent unwanted attentions were becoming even harder than ever to endure. He was badgering her repeatedly to renew her contract, and this evening he had drunk freely, and she could see his temper mounting at her continued refusal. Now, dinner over and guests dispersing, he'd renewed the subject in the middle of the hotel lobby.

'No,' she said carefully, 'it's nothing to do with more money. I simply don't wish to extend my contract any further. I've been very appreciative of it, naturally—'

'That's not the message you're giving out.' Karl cut across her brusquely.

Tight-lipped, Celeste refused to react. She knew very well that the cause of his pique was nothing to do with her not renewing her contract—it was because she wasn't going to do what Monique Silva had done: show her 'appreciation' in bed.

Anger flashed across Karl's face. 'Who the hell do you think you are?' he demanded. 'Models are ten cents a dozen!'

'As I say,' she repeated tightly, 'I've been very appreciative of the opportunity to represent the Blonde range of Reiner Visage, but—'

'But nothing!' He cut across her again. His face was set petulantly. 'I've done you favours! Now it's payback time! You damn well *know* what I want!'

He grabbed at her arm, closing his fingers around it. She halted, turning an icy gaze on him.

'Take your hand off me,' she bit out, jaw clenched. When he made no move to do so, she simply lifted his hand off her and stepped away. 'Good*night,* Mr Rainer,' she said decisively, and turned to go.

Infuriated, and despite the presence of other people in the lobby, he lurched at her, grabbing at her wrist again, yanking her round forcibly. His face was contorted in fury.

'Don't walk off, you stuck-up little bitch! Who the hell do you think you are? Behaving like a goddamn nun!' he snarled at her.

The alcoholic fumes of his breath reached her. His voice was loud and carrying.

'I can pick and choose any model I want—you hear me? And they'll be *grateful!* Girls like you put out for anyone who'll hire you! And since I've hired you you'll damn well put out for *me!* You're no different! You're just a two-bit whore like every other model!'

Celeste gasped in shock. For a second she could not move. Then, behind her, a voice cut through.

'Let her go,' it said. It was arctic. 'Let her go and get out of here before I throw you out onto the pavement.'

Karl's head swivelled. 'Who the hell are *you?*' he snarled slurringly.

Rafael did not answer him. He simply yanked Karl's hand away, then took his shoulder and elbow in a punishing grip and frogmarched him to the door, ejecting him onto the pavement.

'If you try and come back in,' he said pleasantly, 'I will pulverise you. Do you understand me?'

He didn't bother to wait for a reply, just went back into the lobby. His eyes went immediately to the frozen figure standing there, her ashen pallor registering her shock. He went up to her.

'Brandy,' he said. 'Don't argue. Then I'll see you home—and don't argue about that either. That charmless jerk is out on the pavement.'

She couldn't respond. Couldn't do anything except stand there, the vile echo of Karl's accusation slicing through her head.

'You're just a two-bit whore like every other model!'

Her face contorted and she felt nausea rise in her throat, foul and choking. Then, from nowhere, her elbow was being taken—not tightly, but firmly—and she was being guided across the lobby and into the hotel bar. Her steps were halting, but she went all the same. Numbness filled her.

Then, as she was helped up onto a bar stool, the numbness was suddenly pierced. Karl Reiner and his vile words disappeared from her consciousness. Replaced, totally, by the realisation of just who it was that was at her side now.

Her eyes flew to the man, tall and lean in a charcoal tailored lounge suit that only emphasised his naturally tanned complexion, who was taking his seat beside her.

Dear God—it was Rafael Sanguardo!

Shock ravined through her. Shock and something much more. Instant awareness, instant consciousness of everything about him that she had sought to suppress these past few days. To force down out of her memory.

Yet he was here now, in all his overwhelming, potent physical presence. Sitting beside her and looking at her with an expression of concern on his face, his dark eyes resting on her.

She hauled her gaze away. She could not cope with this—not now. Not after Karl Reiner's vile outburst. She could feel herself start to shake.

Immediately she heard Rafael Sanguardo speak. 'It's all right. He's gone. And he won't be coming back.'

He spoke with certainty, and an underlying grimness. Her eyes lifted to him again.

But he was not looking at her. He had turned his head to address the barman. 'Two brandies, please.'

As he gave his order he made a notable effort to control his emotions. They were surging strongly. One was an impulse to stride right out onto the pavement, seize hold of the jerk who had said what he had to the ashen-faced, shaken figure beside him and slam his fist into his foul-mouthed face. It took him aback, just how strong that urge was. A wave of protectiveness swept over him.

No one's going to hurl that kind of abuse at her!

The protectiveness he was feeling was almost overpowering... But him slamming his fist into her abuser was not what she needed right now! What she needed was to stop shaking, to pull out of the shocked state she was clearly in after that vicious little scene back there with Karl Reiner.

He knew who the man was, all right. Just as he now knew the name of the woman who had been dominating his thoughts ever since he'd laid eyes on her.

Celeste Philips—that was her name. It had taken little effort to discover it, courtesy of the organisers of the charity fashion show, simply by describing her. After that her professional bio had been easy to find via her agency. She was currently contracted to Reiner Visage—of which cosmetics company the unlovely Karl Reiner was President. Nor had it taken much digging to uncover Karl Reiner's even more unlovely reputation for pursuing the models he contracted.

A reputation that the ugly incident just now more than amply confirmed.

The two glasses of brandy were placed in front of him and he slid one towards Celeste.

'Drink it down,' he instructed. 'You're in shock.'

But Celeste gave a quick, jerky shake of her head. 'No— no brandy.' Her voice was slightly high-pitched. In her head she could hear Karl's foul words snarling at her again. Hear his vile accusation…

She fought to stay calm, at least on the surface. Inside was different…

'Coffee, then—you need something. You're white as a sheet.'

She lifted her face, made herself look at the man who had rescued her. The man she couldn't get out of her head. Who was now here, beside her, dominating her consciousness. 'I'm fine. It was just—' She stopped. Swallowed painfully.

'Damn,' said Rafael feelingly. 'I should have hit him. Trouble is…' his voice was deadpan '…I might have spoilt his looks.'

For a moment Celeste was on a knife-edge. Then the balance tipped, giving her a safety net, letting her pull herself together. The laconically uttered insult to the drunken, obnoxious Karl had retrieved her sufficiently for her to manage to find the darkly wry humour clearly intended in the remark.

She bit her lip. 'That's a low blow,' she heard herself murmur.

'The lower the better,' Rafael agreed. 'Low enough to… ah…quell his unwanted ardour.'

She gave a shaky smile, not quite meeting his eyes. She might be pulling out of the shock of what Karl had snarled at her, but that only meant she was now having to cope with this completely unanticipated encounter with Rafael Sanguardo. And cope she must—somehow.

And she must start with the most important priority. Gratitude.

She lifted her eyes again. 'Thank you,' she said. 'Thank you for what you did back there.'

For just a moment, as her eyes met his, she felt weak—as weak as a kitten. The blood seemed to be flooding back into her ashen cheeks, heating them. She could not drag her gaze away—his eyes were holding her...holding her as if there was a physical link between them...as if they were bound together...

She saw something shift at the back of his eyes—his dark, basalt-black eyes. Something that seemed to set every nerve-ending in her body jangling.

Then, with a quick movement of his head, he broke the moment. *'De nada,'* he said lightly. His tone of voice changed. 'So, coffee?' he said enquiringly. 'Or tea, maybe? Isn't that what the English drink to settle their nerves?'

'China tea would be lovely, thank you,' she assented, grateful for something so normal. She needed to feel normal again—needed it badly.

As Rafael Sanguardo relayed her request to the barman she felt the backwash of what Karl had said to her start to fade. Her state of shock was ebbing, and so, too, finally, was the sense of incessant strain she'd been under all evening. But even as it ebbed a new emotion replaced it—the shimmering awareness of the man beside her.

Who had appeared out of nowhere to wrest Karl Reiner off her—

'I don't understand,' she heard herself say. 'How did you come to be here like this?'

There was bewilderment in her voice.

'I've been meeting one of my UK CEOs for dinner,' Rafael replied. 'But I have to say...' His tone of voice changed again, and his gaze rested on her. 'I now understand the meaning of that English proverb that it is an ill wind that blows no one any good.'

He looked at her, but Celeste was blank. Rafael enlightened her.

'Even though I would not wish Karl Reiner on anyone, at least he has given me the opportunity not only to be of some small service to you—he has also provided exactly the opportunity I have been wanting to take since the weekend.' He paused deliberately, still looking at her. 'To see you again,' he said.

A troubled expression lit her face.

He saw it and said, his voice low, 'Would that be so very unwelcome to you?'

She bit her lip. She wanted to find some way—a polite, considerate way, especially after his rescuing her from Karl—of telling him that what he wanted was impossible... just impossible!

Rafael saw her silence, needed to know if there was one reason that would be an immovable obstacle for him.

'Is there someone else in your life right now?'

She swallowed, her expression still troubled. 'No, but—' She halted, not knowing what to say. How to say it.

Her hesitation was visible. A hideous thought speared Rafael's head. His expression darkened. 'Karl Reiner,' he began, his voice harsh, 'is he—?'

'No! Dear God, *no!*'

Her rebuff was so instant, so vehement, that it could only be true. Relief flooded through Rafael. If for a moment he'd thought that that despicable piece of ordure had any kind of *anything* with her—

'Gracias a Dios!' he said feelingly.

'How could you think—?' She broke off, shuddering.

Of course she had nothing to do with Karl Reiner in that way! Someone like her would never, *never* think of such a liaison! Hadn't she reacted strongly enough back there in the lobby to convince him of that? Her shock and disgust had been palpable.

He reached for his brandy, and as he took a mouthful an image formed in his mind. Madeline—Madeline being on the receiving end of what Karl Reiner had thrown at Celeste.

She'd have laughed. Laughed in his face, told him, 'In your dreams!' and walked off. Then she'd have regaled Rafael with it in bed. She'd have been totally unfazed by it, totally unaffected—she would have thought Reiner merely physically repellent, not repulsively offensive!

But Madeline was cut from completely different material from the woman at his side now. The woman who was cupping one slender hand around a teacup from which a delicate oriental fragrance was coiling upwards, stirring it with a silver teaspoon, focussed only on her task. He watched her for a moment, all thought of Madeline deleted as Celeste stirred her tea, inhaling the scent, and seemed visibly to calm herself.

'Better?' he asked quietly.

She nodded, lifting the cup to her lips to take a tiny sip of the hot liquid.

He let her be, contenting himself with looking at her. Her beauty, seen again after a space of days, was etching itself on his retinas. Tonight she was wearing a knee-length cocktail dress in eau de Nil, high cut at the neckline, with short cap sleeves. A jade necklace and earrings were her jewellery. Her hair was dressed differently, in a more complex style with braids and loops, but still worn up. An impulse went through him—a longing to see that incredible pale hair loosed from its confines, flowing like a silvery river over her naked alabaster shoulders…

He pulled his mind back from such impulses, focussing now on her features. Her perfect beauty was just the same as it had been when he'd seen her walking down the stairs at that charity event. A beauty that moved him so strangely—so strongly.

And so, too, did the other quality that had made him watch her then, as it did now.

That sense of aloneness—apartness. As if she moved in the world but was not fully part of it. As if it could not touch her.

What had she said about the stars? That they were very far away...

As she is.

His expression changed. *But I will get close to her. With me she will not be alone, apart. I will draw her to me! Woo her and win her!*

And he must make the most of this opportunity to begin his journey to that destination. She was here, beside him, and that, surely, was a start.

'Tell me,' he said, his voice holding in it nothing but quiet concern, 'how is it that you were with Karl Reiner tonight if he is so repugnant to you? I know that you are the face of Blonde Visage, but—'

She lifted her face sharply. 'How do you know that?'

He gave a half laugh. 'I could say that your face is your giveaway,' he said lightly, 'but I have to confess that, since fashion magazines are not my usual reading matter, I found it out from your agency.'

Her face worked. 'Why were you asking?' she demanded. But there was no need to ask. She knew. Rafael Sanguardo had shown his interest in her—she had been naive to think that just because she had walked away from him the other evening it would not be possible for a man of his means to find out a great deal about her!

His expression was deliberately transparent. 'I make no secret of the fact that I want to get to know you better, Celeste.'

It was strange to hear her name on his lips—a name she hadn't told him. She would have preferred him never to know, so that she could slip back into the shadows of life where she dwelt. But it was too late for that. All she could do now was hold him at bay, make it clear to him that whatever he was hoping for could not be.

'So why did you have to be in Reiner's unpalatable company?' Rafael pursued.

She made herself give a slight shrug. 'I'm still under contract, so it's unavoidable. Tonight he was a guest of one of the fashion magazines he places a great deal of advertising with—that was his excuse for me having to be here.'

'Excuse?'

She gave another shrug, not meeting his eyes, focussing only on the cup in front of her. 'You heard what he wants. He made it plain enough.' A sudden thought struck her, and without realising it she lifted her face to look at him.

'What you did—back there—will he make trouble for you?' There was concern in her voice. 'He could do you for assault—'

'He can try,' said Rafael.

And there was something about the way he said it that made Celeste realise that Karl—or anyone—would be very, very foolish to attempt to make trouble for Rafael Sanguardo. There was a toughness about him that was unmistakable.

But there was chivalry, too, she acknowledged. Even if his intervention *had* proved opportune for him, allowing him to do what he was doing now. Getting to know her—

But it's no use—no use at all. Nothing can come of it—nothing!

That was all she had to remember. And she should act on it right now. She should get to her feet, thank him once again and then go home—home to her little flat in Notting Hill: the fruit of her years of modelling, her quiet haven, where she could be apart from the hectic round of her career. Apart and alone.

The way she had to be.

Because nothing else was possible...would ever be possible...

She was condemned to the solitary life she led.

But Rafael Sanguardo was speaking again, interrupting her troubled thoughts. 'What about for you?' he was asking, that note of concern still evident in his deep, accented voice. 'Will it make things difficult?'

She gave another shrug. 'I've only got a few weeks left to run on my contract, and there's little he can do in real terms. I most definitely will *not* be resigning! Oh, there'll probably be some gossip—I dare say some of the people I work with will hear about it. But he has a reputation already, so it will hardly be a surprise.'

Rafael frowned. 'If you had warning of his reputation, why did you take the contract?'

She gave yet another shrug. 'He was involved with one of the other models under contract, so I thought he would leave me alone—which he did, by and large, until now. And the reason I wanted the contract in the first place was simple.' She looked straight at him, giving him the courtesy of an honest answer, for surely he deserved no less after his rescue of her. 'It paid well,' she said.

She lifted up her cup, took a mouthful of tea, breaking her gaze. Then she set down her cup again, looked at him once more. She swallowed, then spoke.

'Modelling is a crowded profession. Often poorly paid. Only a few make it to the very top. I won't be one of them, I know, but I've not done badly—for which I'm grateful,' she allowed. 'Anyway, it's the only way I know of to make money—'

She stopped, and for a moment—just a moment—there was an emptiness in her gaze. As if she had been scoured hollow.

Then it was gone.

Yet in its aftermath there seemed to Rafael to be the residue of something lingering. Unsettling. He wanted to banish it.

He took another mouthful of his brandy, feeling its

warmth filling him. 'It seems to me you know about astronomy,' he said.

He'd lightened his tone deliberately. Yet his attempt to lighten the atmosphere seemed to have failed. Her throat tensed; a shadow occluded her eyes. Memory oozed within her of the way she had first gazed desperately up at the heavens, wanting only to be part of them. Incorporeal. Free from her body…

Then she forced the memory from her. He'd obviously only made the remark as a conversational gambit—she must treat it as such.

'Hard to make a living at that,' she answered. 'And I am the rankest amateur!' she added lightly.

Rafael smiled across at her. 'Yet your name is ideally suited for a career in astronomy, no?' She looked blank, and he enlightened her. 'Celeste—celestial?' he said.

His eyes rested on her, drinking her in.

And that is her aura, too—celestial. As if the impurities and imperfections of the world below the stars are nothing to do with her! As if she moves through this world apart from everyone else, everything else, untouched by anything that seeks to stain her…

In his head he heard Karl Reiner's sordid accusation. If ever there was a woman who was an unlikely target for such foul names it was this one!

She was looking at him, a slight expression of surprise in her clear grey-blue eyes. 'Do you know, that's never struck me?' she said. 'Celeste and celestial…'

His own smile deepened. Absently she noticed how it curved the lines around his mouth, made his basalt-black eyes lighten. Noticed even more the way it seemed to make her breath catch. Made her want to do nothing more than go on sitting here, beside him, being with him—

No! She mustn't! It was pointless—useless! Talking to him about anything—anything at all—had no purpose! She was calmer now, recovered from that horrible scene out in the lobby, and so she must go—leave—go home to the life she had. A life that had no place for Rafael Sanguardo in it. No place for any kind of relationship with anyone.

She nerved herself to take her leave. To terminate this conversation that could go nowhere—nowhere at all! But he was speaking to her yet again, clearly intent on keeping her in conversation.

'So what first got you interested in astronomy?' Rafael asked.

Deliberately he kept his question casual—nothing more than the kind of enquiry anyone might make in social conversation. A safe topic under whose aegis to do what he most wanted to do—set her at her ease. Stop her tensing all the time. Make her comfortable talking with him. Make the most of the opportunity this evening had presented so that he could move on to inviting her out to dinner, and then from there to where he wanted to be—making love to her.

Her arms around me, clinging to me, her mouth opening to mine, my hands curving around the bare column of her back, her hair loosened, streaming like a silver banner across the pillows, her body warm and yielding to desire...

He felt the power of his own imagination, his own desire, kick through him. Surely she must feel it, too? Surely she must? Wasn't she starting to thaw to him, little by little? Slowly—oh, so slowly—but it was starting to happen, he was sure of it.

Then, as he finished his question, before his eyes he saw her face change. Closed.

Closed completely, as if a shutter had come down.

'I don't remember,' she said. Her voice was quelling. This time there could be no allowances for his simply making conversation. This was a subject that she must terminate—now. Just as she must terminate this encounter. She must go home right now.

Rafael's eyes narrowed minutely at her stony reaction. What had just happened? The change was total. He saw her reach for her teacup, lift it with a jerking movement and take a mouthful of the pale green fragrant liquid. Then she set the cup down with another jolt. Her eyes swivelled to his.

'Thank you so much for the tea, Señor Sanguardo. And thank you for intervening back there. It was very good of you.' She spoke rapidly, in clipped tones. Clipped, impersonal tones that went with the totally closed expression on her face.

He could see her total withdrawal happening in front of his eyes.

She's gone away again—back into that separate space she lives in. The one she uses to keep the rest of the world at bay.

She was getting to her feet, slipping gracefully off the high bar stool.

'Thank you so much,' she said again, her tone formal. She picked up her clutch bag from the bar surface and bestowed a tight, perfunctory smile on him again.

Rafael got to his feet as she did. 'I will see you home,' he announced.

Again, that look of immediate wariness—more than wariness...alarm—flared in her eyes.

'Purely and solely,' he continued, 'for the purposes of ensuring that you do not risk any further unwanted attention from the uncharming Mr Reiner. My car is outside, and it is no trouble, I assure you.' He looked down at her. His eyes were steady, their message clear. 'I will see you safely to your home and then leave you. Does that meet with your agreement?'

Celeste opened her mouth. She wanted to say, *No, it can't possibly meet with my agreement! I can't want to spend the slightest further amount of time with you because there is no point—absolutely and totally no point! I am not going to let you get to know me better and I am not going to have anything more to do with you and that is all there is to it!*

But she didn't say it. A sudden vision of Karl Reiner waiting outside her flat assailed her. However reluctant she might be to allow this magnetic, disturbing man who had behaved so chivalrously to drive her home, it was preferable to encountering Karl Reiner again—drunken and angry and still trying to press his hateful attentions on her.

Then, without any answer from her at all, she felt Rafael Sanguardo's strong hand cup lightly around her elbow and guide her out of the bar. It was only a light, courteous touch, but she was vividly aware of it. He dropped his hand the moment she seemed to be going the way he wanted her to—which was across the lobby and out onto the pavement. A hovering car glided to the kerb, and then a chauffeur was opening the passenger door for her and she was getting in.

'Where to?' Rafael asked her as he took his place beside her.

With a flurry of consternation Celeste realised she was going to have to tell him where she lived. Well, if he'd found out who she was, then he'd be perfectly capable of finding out where she lived as well. So she gave her address, and the car started to make its way westward out of Mayfair towards Park Lane.

It would take a good fifteen minutes at least to reach Notting Hill, Celeste knew, and in the meantime she had better make anodyne conversation to prevent Rafael Sanguardo getting any other ideas about how to pass the time in the back of his car...

'What part of South America do you come from, Mr Sanguardo?' she heard herself asking. Her tone was no more than politely interested.

He glanced at her. There was amusement in his eyes. 'Am I to take it that you've been making enquiries about me in return?' he asked.

Damn, she thought, *I walked into that one!*

'One of my fellow models the other evening at the charity show mentioned it,' she replied, making her voice as unconcerned as she could.

Did she, now? Rafael thought. *And does that mean that*

you'd asked her? A ripple of satisfaction went through him. She was not as studiedly indifferent to him as she was trying to make out. How long, he wondered, before she finally admitted that? Before she finally started to lower her guard to him?

But whenever that happened—and it *would* happen; he had set his mind to it, and nothing in the intervening days since seeing her walk down that marble staircase, captivating him with her opalescent beauty, had changed his mind on that—it was not happening now.

Her guard was sky-high. A guard consisting of polite attentiveness and the kind of impersonal conversation she could have with anyone at all. Well, he reminded himself, it was better than her doing her disappearing act again, and he would make the most of it.

'She was a little out,' he answered. 'My country of origin is Maragua, which is in Central America.'

He could see her give a little frown in the passing street lights as the car drew out into Park Lane.

'I thought Managua was the capital of Nicaragua?' she commented.

'It is. Which is why my country, *Maragua,* is so often overlooked. It's very small—hardly larger than El Salvador—and similarly has only a Pacific coastline.'

'I don't think I've really ever heard of it,' Celeste said apologetically.

'*De nada*—not many Europeans have,' he said. 'Which, overall, is probably a good thing.' His voice was edged. 'After all, the reason most developing countries are known about in the Western world is their wars and disasters! Fortunately we have few—though like all Pacific Rim countries we are subject to earthquakes.'

'Because the Pacific Ocean's floor is moving under the continental plates,' she acknowledged. 'Does that mean you have volcanoes, too?'

He nodded his head. 'One or two—fortunately inactive.'

He paused. 'Your geology is as good as your astronomy, it seems.'

His eyes rested on her expectantly. He felt another ripple of satisfaction. Beauty, even so notable as hers, was one thing, but it was inadequate on its own. Her stargazing had told him that she was informed and intelligent, and here was further proof.

'I like plate tectonics,' she answered. 'It makes sense of so much.'

'The whole planet earth is a living jigsaw—endlessly changing, endlessly renewing itself.' Rafael paused. 'I find that quite encouraging. If even the ground beneath our feet can change, then so can we. We can make ourselves anew.'

She looked at him. Her eyes flickered. His words echoed in her head. *We can make ourselves anew.*

For just a second she could feel something flare inside her—then it died. Crushed by the weight of the past. The past that was always her present. And her future...the only future possible for her.

Feeling a stone suddenly in her chest, she turned her head to look out of the car window. They had reached Hyde Park Corner and were turning into the park now.

Rafael indicated with his hand. 'What is that enormous house there, do you know?' he asked. He wanted her to keep talking to him—not slip away into that separate world she inhabited, shutting him out.

But she answered readily enough. 'Oh, that's Apsley House,' she said. 'It's the London home of the Duke of Wellington—you know, the Battle of Waterloo. Well, his descendants anyway. It's always known as Number One, London. I suppose it's because it's the premier private residence in London.'

If she was gabbling, she didn't care. This kind of innocuous exchange was all she could cope with. It blocked those tormenting words he'd said—*We can make ourselves anew.*

Anguish gripped her. *But I can't—I can't make myself anew!
It's impossible—impossible!*

His voice relieved her. 'Is that the Serpentine?' he asked,
glimpsing a dark mass of water to one side of the car as they
cut across the park.

'Yes,' she answered. The stone was back in her chest. She
launched into relating everything she knew about the Serpentine, then moved on to Rotten Row as they crossed it.

'It's still a bridle path,' she said. 'In the nineteenth century it was very fashionable for the upper classes to ride
their horses there.'

Somehow she managed to make the subject of Victorian high society last till they reached her flat, and as the
car pulled up along the quiet kerbside she turned to Rafael.

'Thank you so much,' she said brightly. 'It really is very
kind of you.'

The chauffeur was holding the door open for her and she
climbed out gracefully. The night air seemed cool after the
interior of the car. Or perhaps it was just because she felt
heated in her blood.

'Please don't get out,' she told Rafael.

'Which is your flat?' he asked, ignoring her and stepping
out onto the pavement.

'Um...second floor,' she said. She was fumbling for her
keys in her clutch.

She'd coped with the car ride, sounding like a tour guide
to London, but her nerves were at breaking point. She had
to get in. Get away from him.

'I'll wait until I see your light come on,' said Rafael.

Relief flooded through her. 'Thank you,' she said. She
hurried up the steps to the front door, opening it with her
key. She turned. He was still standing there. 'Goodnight,
Mr Sanguardo,' she said, her smile flickering uncertainly.

For a moment she just went on standing there, looking
at him. Letting the impact he made on her retinas be absorbed into her.

'Goodnight, Celeste,' he answered. He gave her a brief nod of farewell and got back into the car. The chauffeur slammed the door and went to the driver's seat.

Celeste went indoors, walking swiftly up to her flat. As she turned the light on and went to the living room windows to see the car pulling away she could feel her heart's hectic beating.

And she knew exactly what had caused it.

Rafael Sanguardo...

His name echoed in her head. Not letting her go.

Later, as she lay in bed, she knew she should get to sleep. She had an early start tomorrow and looking haggard was not acceptable for a model—yet she lay sleepless all the same.

Memories from the evening circled in her mind. Not the stressful dinner with Karl Reiner, but the time she had spent with Rafael Sanguardo. It was his words that kept playing in her head.

We can make ourselves anew...

Her eyes stared out into the darkness of her bedroom.

Can we? Can we make ourselves anew?

But the question was hollow. Its flavour bitter. And into her head came more words. Karl Reiner's...

Anguish gripped her.

CHAPTER FOUR

CELESTE WONDERED THE next day whether Rafael Sanguardo would try to get in touch, but there was nothing from him. She told herself she was glad—must be glad—for there could be no future for her with him in it.

So why, then, did she keep thinking about him, replaying her time with him? There was no point! Yet, berate herself as she might, she could not get him out of her head. Even when she was enduring the final photographic sessions under her Reiner Visage contract he was there, dominating her consciousness, her thoughts. Vivid and potent. And as disturbing as ever. As tormenting as ever.

His sculpted features, the mobile mouth, the sable hair, the dark obsidian eyes, the deep, accented voice...

And then she was back to the beginning again, trying to get those images out of her mind. Trying to move on beyond the completely pointless question of what it was about him that was getting to her.

Because it doesn't matter why! It's irrelevant—totally irrelevant! It changes nothing! Nothing at all! If he tries to get in touch with me again I'll just say no, that's all. The way I always do. Always... Because nothing else is possible. Nothing.

In her eyes a shadow passed. An old, familiar shadow... And with it came the clenching of her stomach, the crawling of her skin.

* * *

Rafael relaxed back in the first-class seat on the plane, a pleasant sense of satisfaction filling him. And anticipation. He'd been in Geneva, raising finance for his latest ventures; with his track record, banks were always eager to meet with him. But his thoughts were not on business now.

An image floated tantalisingly in his mind. Pale, beautiful...*celestial*...

He'd given Celeste time and space since delivering her to her flat, but now he was going to make his next move. Would she respond? he wondered. Or would she try and evade him? His mind flickered over the situation. She was not immune to him—he could tell that with every male molecule in his body—yet she was holding him at bay. Why, since she had admitted she was not involved with anyone else, he could not fathom. She gave no impression of trying to play him, and her evasiveness seemed totally genuine. But why be evasive in the first place?

His eyes narrowed as he thought it through. Maybe it was because of men like Karl Reiner. If he was the norm for men in the world of fashion and modelling she moved in, he could understand Celeste's evasiveness. To be treated as that all-time prime jerk had treated her would make anyone cautious about accepting attentions from men.

Well, he was no Karl Reiner, and he would win her confidence and make her realise he was nothing like that! Soon—very soon now—he would convince her that all he wanted from her was what he knew with every instinct she wanted, too...

Time together—with him.

His pleasant sense of anticipation intensified.

Celeste's phone was ringing. It was Sunday evening and she was ironing. She was keeping busy—deliberately so. Anything to keep Rafael Sanguardo out of her head! Her work with Reiner Visage had finally ended, to her relief, and since then she'd thrown herself into a round of activity while waiting for another modelling assignment to come up.

So far she'd given herself a whole set of beauty treatments and set a challenging exercise schedule—runs in Holland Park, yoga, Pilates and dance classes. And she had a full medical assessment booked for a few days' time as well, with blood tests and body scans.

It was not just for the sake of her modelling career that she paid such attention to herself. A shadow dimmed her eyes. She needed not only to stay beautiful but to stay fit and healthy. She would not go the way of her poor, stricken mother...

A familiar sadness filled her, squeezing her heart. She had promised her mother she would not suffer the same terrible fate that had befallen her—forewarned was forearmed, and regular check-ups were routine for her.

Now, as she folded a pillowcase and reached for the next one to iron, she let the phone go to the answer machine. As the caller started speaking she froze.

She did not need to ask whose was the distinctive accented voice.

How did he get my phone number? was her first thought, swiftly discarded. He knew her name and address—easy enough to find her landline number! At least, she thought with a sense of relief, he hadn't phoned her mobile, so hopefully he didn't have that number.

She listened to him speak, the iron poised in her hand. The deep tones wove into her senses almost before she caught the gist of what he was saying.

'I was wondering whether you might like to have dinner with me some time. I'm in the UK this coming week—let me know what evening would suit you. You can reach me on the following number.'

He gave the number—a London landline—and hung up. He didn't bother, she noticed, saying who he was.

He knows I know...

As the phone went quiet again she stared out across her living room. The TV was on in one corner, playing an old black-and-white movie. She did not see the images—only the inner image in her head. Rafael Sanguardo in all his disturbing, unsettling, lean good looks.

Why is he getting to me?

The question formed again, as it had been doing since she had first seen him watching her. And it was just as unanswered. As unanswerable.

And all the more disturbing for it.

The following day she was booked for a catalogue shoot—it wasn't the most glamorous of modelling work, but it paid solidly and Celeste welcomed it now she was without the Reiner contract. When she got back to her flat the entrance hall contained a vase with a huge bouquet of white lilies in it, their scent filling the small space. A gilt-edged card with her name on it was attached to the lavish wrapping.

Upstairs, she opened the envelope. The card said simply 'Rafael'. Nothing more than that. Her face set, she put the extravagant bouquet on the dining table. Behind her set expression, though, her thoughts were tumbling around.

They resolved into a single question.

What am I going to do about him?

The question stayed with her all the evening.

So did the scent of the lilies, pervading the living room, the whole flat. It was a scent she could not avoid, nor ignore. Just like the single, simple question hovering in her head. She knew perfectly well what answer was required. Go on ignoring Rafael Sanguardo, whatever he did.

It got increasingly hard during the rest of the week. He phoned again, leaving another message—more or less a repetition of the first—and the following day yet another bouquet of flowers arrived. These were quite different from the exotic, opulent lilies—just a slender posy of freesias in delicate pastel colours, with a sweet, fresh scent. The card held just a question: 'Perhaps you prefer these flowers?'

She put them in a vase on her dressing table in her bedroom, so their delicate scent would not be drowned by the heady lilies. But it meant that wherever she was in her flat there was a reminder of Rafael Sanguardo.

At least her days were very busy with the catalogue shoot, and she was glad of that. Less glad, though, to return home and find yet another floral tribute had arrived from Rafael Sanguardo. This time it was a cluster of tiny rosebuds in the palest blush-pink. She put them beside the freesias. If he kept going like this she could open a flower shop, she thought.

But his phone call that evening told her she was going to have a respite. He simply left a message saying that he was flying to the Far East for a week, but would be back in London thereafter.

'Perhaps your schedule will allow you some evenings out then,' he said. 'I'll phone you.'

He seemed totally unperturbed by her persistent lack of reply to him. Yet the deep, accented tones of his voice seemed to linger in her consciousness long after she'd deleted the message.

She eyed the phone warily. Maybe she should simply call him and tell him that he was wasting his time. But even that seemed an ordeal. *Why can't he just take the hint—get the message from the fact I'm not phoning him back? Why can't he just disappear out of my life?*

But even as she thought that she felt a strange little pang go through her. A pang that was the most disturbing reaction of all...

Thoughts and emotions crowded into her head. If Rafael Sanguardo was going to be abroad, then maybe she should plan to do likewise. Go somewhere different from where he was going to be—somewhere she could try and get him out of her mind.

Resolved, the next morning she went to her agency with a request for a foreign location shoot.

Her booker looked put out. 'Just because you ditched

Reiner Visage, it doesn't mean you can get the work you want at the drop of a hat!' he pointed out tartly. Then he relented. 'OK, OK—I know. Creepy Karl's enough to make anyone run a mile! Hmm...let's see. Hang on for a mo—I'll put some calls in.'

He picked up his phone and Celeste wandered off to sit on one of the group of white leather chairs nearby. She'd just sat down when the door from the street was pushed open and someone came in. It was a model Celeste didn't recognise. She was very fair-skinned, with hair as blonde as her own. She looked young, still in her teens, and unsure what to do. One of the bookers greeted her, and she went up to him eagerly, sitting herself down, her long, thin legs splaying like a newborn foal's.

Celeste looked at her. The girl could have been herself all those years ago. Memory pierced. Sharp—like a needle under the skin. Finding the nerve beneath. She picked up a magazine and busied herself with its contents. A few moments later her own booker called her across.

'Can you do Hawaii? Five days, end of next week? One of the models booked for it has just discovered she's pregnant and wants out!'

Celeste nodded. Hawaii was definitely far enough away to get some perspective and would suit her very well.

Her booker finished telling her the details and she got up to go. As she did so the very young new model got up as well. Her face was shining.

'Oh, that's brilliant! Thank you!' she said excitedly to her booker.

She got to the door just before Celeste, and held it open for her. As they stepped out onto the pavement Celeste said in a friendly voice, 'Got a casting?'

The girl beamed. 'My first one! Tomorrow! It's for skincare. I'm just terrified I'll wake up tomorrow with a zit!'

Celeste laughed. 'Drink nothing but water for the rest of

the day,' she advised, half joking. 'Who's the client?' she asked, just to be friendly.

But when the girl answered Celeste's expression changed.

'Reiner Visage,' breathed the girl. 'They're ever so posh! I can't afford any of their stuff myself! Do you think I can get some free samples?' she asked ingenuously.

Celeste didn't answer. Her face was grave. The girl looked so young— *Young and naive and vulnerable...*

Memory's needle went under her skin again.

'Listen,' she said, sounding serious, 'if you do get picked, please be careful. Karl Reiner's nickname is Creepy Karl, and he's earned it!'

She debated whether to tell the girl about the hassle she herself had had, then decided not to. The odds were against her getting a Reiner contract at her very first casting, and she was obviously so thrilled right now that Celeste didn't want to spoil the moment with an unnecessary warning.

She fished in her bag for a scrap of paper, scrawled her name and mobile number on it and gave it to the girl. 'I'm Celeste Philips. Let's have a coffee some time,' she said, her voice friendly again.

The girl's eyes shone. 'Oh, that would be brill—thanks! I don't know any other models yet. My flatmates all work in offices. I'm Louise, by the way—Louise Foreman,' she said.

'Well, good luck, Louise,' Celeste said, refraining from adding, *But not tomorrow.*

'I'll put your name and number in my phone right away,' Louise said happily. 'Thank you ever so much! I can't wait to tell my mates I've got a casting!'

She trotted off, busy with her phone. Celeste watched her go. *Was I really ever that young?* she thought. *That eager?*

But she had been. Of course she had. After all, modelling had been going to make her fortune. The fortune she'd wanted so much...

Like a guillotine, she sliced down the steel door in her

head that she kept forever locked. Seeing that young girl, so like herself once, had let it start to open.

But it wasn't just the young model who had turned the key in that door. Like an unwelcome intruder, Rafael Sanguardo's image formed in her mind, as disturbing now as it had been from the start.

What power does he have to do that? Why does he get to me the way he does? Why can't I just delete him and never think about him again?

The answer was as disturbing as the man himself.

And one thing was for sure: Rafael Sanguardo's image did not come with a delete button…

Rafael's brow was furrowed in concentration as he focussed on the figures his laptop screen was displaying. Calculations ran rapidly through his head.

'Sorry to disturb you, but Miss Philips has just turned the corner.'

His driver's voice interrupted his concentration, but he looked up at once.

'Thank you,' he said crisply, shutting his laptop lid. He twisted his head very slightly to look out of the window of his parked car. He saw her at once.

She was wearing jeans, a grey sweater and sneakers. Her hair was in a long plait to one side, and she had a capacious leather bag on her shoulder. She looked fresh and fit, her face without a trace of make-up, clean and clear, her figure slender and long-legged.

Rafael watched her a moment, analysing his feelings. They had not changed. Even casually dressed, as she was now, she had an impact on him that went straight to the same place as when she was dressed to the nines. Holding his gaze totally. Filling his vision.

He got out of the car, watching her register his presence. Watching her stop dead.

Casually, he walked up to her. 'You really do take evasion to the limits, don't you?' he said pleasantly.

Celeste glared at him. 'What are you doing here?' Her heart had started to slug, and she hated him for it. Hated herself.

'Asking you to dinner,' Rafael answered, unconcerned by her aggrieved tone.

The grey-blue eyes flashed. 'Thank you—but no, thank you,' she said. Then she frowned. 'I thought you were in the Far East?'

'I came back early,' Rafael said smoothly. His voice changed. 'I found I didn't want to be away.' He paused. 'From you,' he finished.

His eyes were resting on her. She was flustered, he could see. More than flustered. Her skin had flushed—that pale, translucent, flawless skin that he wanted to reach out a hand and smooth with the tips of his fingers…

Her skin betrays her—her own body betrays her…

Celeste Philips could stonewall him all she liked. She could ignore his calls—ignore *him*—but what she could not do was hide her response to him.

'So,' he went on, his voice still smooth, his eyes still resting on her, 'are you busy tonight?'

He saw her square her shoulders.

'Look,' she began, 'I really don't think—'

'Then don't,' he interrupted.

His voice wasn't smooth any more. Something had changed within it—something that reached into her, past all her defences.

'Don't think, Celeste. Just smile and say, *That would be lovely!* And then I will smile, too, and we'll agree what time I'll send the car for you, and then you'll go up to your flat and spend the next couple of hours making yourself even more beautiful than you look right now. And I will drive off and bury myself in work, the way I've been doing since I last saw you, because that's the only way I've kept functioning.' He drew breath, his eyes never leaving hers. 'So, that's all agreed, then. The car will be here for you at eight.'

She opened her mouth again. He laid a single long finger against it, silencing her. He felt her lips tremble beneath his touch.

'Dinner,' he said, holding her gaze with his—a troubled gaze that told him of her wariness, her mixed emotions. 'Just dinner, Celeste. Simple, pleasant, undemanding. You can get to know me a little more, and I you. And if we agree that, yes, we enjoy each other's company—after all...' the slightest tug pulled at his mouth '...we share a fondness for astronomy and geology, and who knows how many other ologies, hmm?—then, and only then, we can decide whether we would like to enjoy more of each other's company. There— is that really so very onerous?'

He dropped his hand. This time she did not open her mouth to speak. She just looked at him, an almost helpless look on her face now, as if she had finally run out of ways to gainsay him.

He took a breath. 'One evening of your life, Celeste. That's all.' He held her eyes, then veiled his own with a dipping of his long black lashes. He turned away, reached for the handle of the car door. 'Eight o'clock, Celeste,' he reminded her.

Then he lowered himself into the rear passenger seat and pulled the door shut. A moment later the car had moved off into the road, leaving Celeste behind, standing motionless on the pavement.

But with a heart-rate that felt as if she'd just sprinted five hundred metres.

Slowly, very slowly, she raised the tips of her fingers to her lips. It seemed to her they could still feel Rafael Sanguardo's cool touch...

CHAPTER FIVE

THE CAR CAME at eight. Celeste could see it from her living room window, pulled over by the kerb. She stared down at it. Was she mad to be doing this?

She knew she was. Mad even to think of doing what she was going to do. Have dinner with Rafael Sanguardo.

But it's only dinner! And I need to do this! I need to use it to tell him that what he wants isn't going to happen! It just isn't!

She picked up her evening bag, headed downstairs to the waiting car. Tension pulled at her as she walked out onto the pavement. Deliberately she had chosen a dove-grey dress with a high neckline and a modest knee-length hem. Her make-up was subdued and her hair was in a neat French pleat.

All the way to the restaurant she strove for calm composure. Tonight she would tell Rafael Sanguardo that his efforts were in vain—that there could be nothing between them.

The restaurant—a double-fronted white stucco house in Knightsbridge—was not one she knew. She was shown into the dining salon and instantly her eyes went to the man who dominated her thoughts...her senses. As she was shown to his table, Rafael got to his feet.

'You came,' he said.

His voice was warm. His gaze warmer. It did things to her that it shouldn't. That she must not allow.

She looked very slightly taken aback at his greeting. 'Did you think I wouldn't?'

He quirked an eyebrow. 'Would it have been so surprising? Given your reluctance?'

She said nothing, only took her place as the chair was drawn out for her. She settled into her seat, accepting the napkin unfurled for her and the pouring of water for her. A pair of menus was discreetly placed on the table, and then they were left alone.

The restaurant was almost full, she could see that instantly, although the tables were skilfully arranged such that none was too close to another and each seemed to have a circle of privacy around it, helped by the copious greenery that adorned the room. The decor was late Victorian, with a lot of dark red.

Rafael saw her looking around. 'A little florid, I agree,' he murmured. 'But the food is outstanding, and I don't think this restaurant features on the fashionista circuit.'

'No,' Celeste said. 'I've not been here before.'

'Good,' said Rafael. 'I'm pleased to be able to offer you a new experience.' He picked up his glass of water. 'To new experiences,' he said.

There was a glint of mordant humour in his dark eyes.

Celeste bit her lip, but did not reply. Rafael reached for the menus, opening one and offering it to Celeste, who took it and busied herself studying it.

It saved her from studying him instead. Which, she knew with a little plunge of her stomach, was what she badly wanted to do. She wanted to study him—take in every one of his features and understand, finally, what it was about him that had such an effect on her. Why him? Why this man?

Why, why, why…?

'Will you eat as little as you did at the charity show?' he asked, making her lift her head from the blurring words on the menu.

She frowned slightly. 'Oh, no—I skipped lunch today, as I was working, so I have a full calorie allowance tonight.'

He nodded. 'So you'll go for the baked Camembert, followed by *confit* of duck, and a very large chocolate mousse with cream to finish—is that it?'

He said it straight-faced, and just for a moment Celeste thought he meant it. Then she saw the glint of humour in his eyes.

'I wish...' she said. She looked quickly at the menu again. 'Undressed prawns, and sole with green vegetables—no sauce.'

'Hmm...really splashing out, I see,' Rafael murmured. 'Do you have any calories to spare for wine?'

'Dry white,' she answered, then promptly wished she hadn't. Rafael Sanguardo was disturbing enough to her without the aid of alcohol...

But he was beckoning the wine waiter and going through the wine list with him in a knowledgeable fashion. Then, their dinner order given and the ritual of the arrival of the wine performed, she was left facing him with no other distractions.

'What do you think of the wine?' Rafael was asking, and she took a grateful sip—that would occupy a few moments of time.

'Very good,' she said, for it was crisp and tart and perfectly chilled.

'I'm glad,' he said. Then, glancing at her, he said, 'I'm saving the champagne for our breakfast in bed tomorrow morning.'

She choked, clunking her wine glass down on the table. As she recovered, her eyes flew to his face. It was completely deadpan. Then, a second later, that glint in his eyes came again.

'It's what you think of me, though, isn't it?' Rafael said. He took a breath, his expression changing. 'You know,' he said slowly, 'I've never met anyone as...as *wary*...as you are.

I'm truly astonished that I've actually finally got you sitting here, of your own free will, having dinner with me.' His eyes rested on her. 'Can it be that you've finally decided I'm safe?'

Celeste blinked, her eyes flaring. *Safe?* Rafael Sanguardo sat there and called himself *safe?* A man who was getting past every defence she possessed? Defences she had never even needed till now!

She pulled herself together. He was giving her the perfect opportunity she was looking for. To inform him, as clearly as was needed, that this was not the start of something—it was the end of it.

'Mr Sanguardo—' she began.

'Rafael,' he corrected.

She couldn't bring herself to say his given name. It would create a level of familiarity that was exactly what she was trying to distance herself from.

'I really do have to make something clear to you,' she went on. She fiddled with the stem of her wine glass, steeling herself. Why was it so hard to say what she had to say? It wouldn't be the first time. Usually it never came to this, because men who were keen on her had backed off long before now—frozen out by her lack of response to their overtures—but from time to time she'd had to spell it out with capital letters. This was definitely one of them.

But it wasn't like any of the earlier times. Because then, she knew, with a hollowing of her insides, it had been no effort at all to say no to what was on offer. Whereas now…

I don't want to say no to him…

The words were in her head before she could stop them, forcing themselves into her consciousness. For the first time she had finally encountered a man to whom her customary rejection to all males was not easy and effortless to make. For the first time she had encountered a man to whom she did not want to say no.

She wanted to give a completely different answer…an answer that was singing in her blood, that had leapt in her eyes the very first moment she had seen him, that was making her want to do nothing more than let her eyes gaze at him, soak him up. Her nerves were tingling in every limb, her heart was beating that much faster, her breathing was unsteady…

Then harsh reality sounded in her head.

But it's no good! I have to say no! I have to say no to Rafael Sanguardo. Because I always have to say no.

How could she ever say anything else when that clinging trail of slime still left its fetid trace across her skin…would always do so…?

I can't escape the past—what I did. And I can never be free of it—never! So what else can I say to any man except no…

And that was exactly what she was going to do now. *Make* herself do.

'I have to be completely honest with you,' she ploughed on. She was looking at him full in the face and he sat back, a veiled look in his eyes. 'This isn't personal, I assure you, but it wouldn't be fair of me to let you think that having dinner like this is in any way…um…well, a date—because it isn't.'

'Why not?' The question cut across her hesitant explication. It was asked with an air of casual curiosity. The veiled look was still in his eyes.

'Well, because—' She stopped.

'Yes?' One dark eyebrow quirked. He picked up his wine glass, holding it in long fingers but not drinking from it. He looked relaxed, unfazed by what she was saying.

'Because I just don't *do* this stuff, that's why,' she said bluntly.

'Ah, "stuff",' he repeated with an air of discovery. 'That's very enlightening. Do, please, elaborate.'

She took a breath. 'Like I said, it isn't personal, but I've made it a rule not to…to… Well, to do what I'm doing now, I guess. Or,' she added pointedly, 'anything else!'

'Such as champagne breakfasts in bed?'

'Yes!'

Rafael responded ruminatively. 'Well, I can understand why, if you move in a world populated by the likes of Karl Reiner, you have that rule, and I regard it as entirely sensible. But, Celeste...'

Now his eyes were unveiled, and she reeled from the expression in them that blazed like a searing fire.

'I am *not* cut from that cloth, and therefore you have absolutely nothing to be wary of in that respect. I had hoped you'd realised that already, but if I have to make it even clearer then I shall!'

'It isn't that. I don't think you're anything like Creepy Karl. It's just—'

'Yes?'

He was back to veiling his gaze again, waiting to hear what she said next. She looked away a moment. Only a glance into the restaurant beyond her. But it went a lot further than that.

Back through time...

Then, slowly, she brought her gaze back to his face.

'I don't date,' she said. 'I don't date and I don't have relationships. Or romances. Or affairs. Or whatever you want to call them. I just...*don't.*'

She could hear the silence. Hear it stretching between them. Keeping them apart.

She saw him set down his wine glass, straighten in his seat, lean towards her. He reached a hand out and covered one of hers, still lying palm-down on the tablecloth. His hand felt warm and strong. He held it for a few seconds only, then released it. It felt cold, suddenly, without his there.

'We'll take it very slowly,' he said.

She shook her head. She felt a heavy weight in it. Yet with a flicker of her mind she knew she did not sense the weight as crushing.

Comforting...

The word formed in her mind and she tried to shake it loose. She must not think that—*must not.*

She heard his voice continue. 'As slowly as continental drift,' he said.

And now his eyes were resting on her, and the expression in them was one she had not seen. It did strange things to her, tightening her throat as if she were about to cry, which made no sense at all.

'Will that be slowly enough for you?' he asked.

She felt her head incline, for the weight it was bearing was too great. Continental drift… A pull of desolation went through her. She had her own version of continental drift.

An island of my own, cut off from the rest of the land—drifting ever further away, taking me with it, taking me away from everything like this. Everything that goes with a man like Rafael Sanguardo…

She wanted to tell him so—tell him that even geological time would not be enough to accomplish what he wanted. But she kept silent.

'Good,' he said. His voice was quiet. Then, in a different tone, he said, 'Ah, I believe this is our food arriving.'

It was, and she was glad. It gave her the chance to pull herself together, to shake loose the weight in her head. What had happened just then she did not know—only that she was glad she was past it. She'd said what she had to say—that his attempt to persuade her into dating him, romancing him, having an affair with him, was not going to work and could not work—and that was the important thing. At least his words had indicated that he wasn't going to try and hustle her, pressurise her or hurry her. And that meant, she realised with a little ripple of relief that carried agitations of its own, that she didn't have to keep her guard sky-high this evening. That she could afford to lower it a little—just a little.

The way I want to…

The realisation was impossible to suppress. And that in itself was disturbing, too. But she was here now. To stand up and leave would be rude, and churlish, and he did not deserve that. It was not his fault that she could not do what he had so openly stated he wanted to do.

He's done nothing wrong—he has not behaved badly. When he intervened over Karl Reiner he was chivalrous and protective. Now he is only being attentive, as he said he wanted to be. There is nothing to fault him.

No, the fault was not in Rafael Sanguardo...

She felt them again—those trailing tendrils that dragged across her skin, the miasma of the mind that she could never banish. Never free herself from. That barred her for ever from what Rafael Sanguardo was offering her.

All I can have of him is this—this brief time with him.

And she must make the most of it! Take what little she could. Put aside, just for now, her endless reserve, for she had made it as clear as she could that there could be nothing between them—nothing more than this.

So slowly, very slowly, she started to feel the tension around her begin to ebb a little. She would have this evening and then go home. Home to her solitary life. The only life she could have.

But until that moment she was here, with Rafael Sanguardo, making conversation with him, safe and innocuous.

'Apparently,' he said, 'this house was owned by a Victorian banker who bankrupted himself aspiring to impress the aristocracy—doubtless those who went riding in Rotten Row, as you described the other evening—but they regarded him as a *parvenu*.'

'You were only supposed to inherit money then,' Celeste commented, 'not make it yourself.'

'That rules me out, then,' Rafael replied, that mordant glint in his eyes again.

'I think,' she answered with a slight frown, 'that if you were foreign it was actually a bit easier to get into high society. No one knew who you were, you see.'

One dark, arched eyebrow quirked. 'Wouldn't I have been

regarded as one up—if that—from a savage native escaped from the jungle?'

'I think you would have been considered exotic,' she said. 'And mysterious.'

And you'd have had Victorian maidens swooning by the dozen...

Rafael gave a laugh, the lines around his mouth deepening.

Make that by the hundreds...

Celeste dragged her mind away. She'd set him clear on what she was not going to do—get involved with him in any way—so she had to stop, *right now,* thinking any thoughts at all that countered that.

But it was hard to sit here, only a few feet away from him, and not think such thoughts. Not to feel again the confusion, the incomprehension, about just why it was that he could make her think such things. Feel such things...

'You make me sound like a character in Dickens,' he replied.

'More like Joseph Conrad, I think. You know—*Nostromo,*' she went on. 'It's a novel set in your part of the world. About a town that has vast mountains of silver and how that wealth tempts everyone. Corrupts many.'

'There was such a mountain,' he told her. 'In Peru. And it tempted and corrupted, and in the end caused the death of many. Including the wretched miners forced to mine it for their masters.' His expression changed. 'It may sound ironic, but it's actually been a blessing that Maragua has very little mineral wealth to exploit, since such exploitation has so seldom been for the benefit of the mass of inhabitants of the countries.'

She looked across at him. 'Is there great poverty still in Maragua?'

'Substantial—but it is diminishing. There was a change in government in Maragua a few years ago,' he continued, clearly approvingly, 'to one that is more moderate, less extreme. It has helped considerably. It understands that prosperity is built on investment—investment in infrastructure, the environment, education, entrepreneurship—and a lot of hard work by everyone, not just the *peones*.'

She looked at him curiously. 'But you live and work in Europe and the USA, don't you?'

'It's where I made my money, yes,' Rafael allowed. 'But the habit of sending remittances home by those working abroad has a long tradition in Latin America and it actually contributes signally to the economy of the region *en masse*. However, at my level those remittances can take the form of specific investments in targeted projects for long-term national benefit. I work closely with several other Maraguans who, like myself, have "made good", and we now intend to grow our native economy and welfare for the benefit of all our fellow citizens.'

'That sounds very…admirable…' Celeste sought for the right word.

He gave a dismissive shrug. 'It makes sound economic sense. Wealth begets wealth—as the Western world learned last century. If the masses become prosperous they drive the economy further upwards in a virtuous circle.'

Celeste frowned. 'But isn't there a danger of pollution and environmental degradation as living standards rise with consumer demand?'

'Yes. Which is why we now focus on sustainable development and reversing the damage that has been done in the past.'

He warmed to his theme, describing reforestation programmes to extend areas of native rainforest, which went hand in hand with developing ecotourism—an area he was investing in himself. Rafael could see her listening attentively, and she asked intelligent, penetrating questions.

Just as Madeline had used to.

Emotion flickered through him. He wanted Celeste to

be completely different from Madeline, yet in this she was proving similar.

Or was she?

He had come to realise that the superb grasp of economics that Madeline possessed, allowing her to soar in the business world, did not extend to being overly concerned about the very issues he was now talking about with Celeste. The shadow in Rafael's eyes changed to something harder—more critical. He could still hear Madeline arguing with him, refuting his enthusiasm for such projects as ecotourism and long-term sustainable development and natural resource conservation.

Her assured, confident voice sounded in his head now. *'Rainforests are a prime capital asset that have to be exploited to get anything useful out of them! You can't hold back economic growth by sentimentalising over a bunch of trees and the monkeys living in them! Get real, Rafe! It's a dog-eat-dog world out there, and we both know it! You and I both came from nowhere, and look at us now! We've made good by following the money—using our talents to get our share of it! Being sentimental would have got us nowhere!'*

He heard her vehement, scornful voice—knowing now, although he had once ignored it, that her callous attitude should have been a warning sign to him long before she had revealed her true character and finished their relationship for good.

Celeste's reaction to his environmental concerns was very different. Sympathetic, enthusiastic, approving. Sharing his values.

His eyes rested on her warmly, darkening momentarily with desire. He wanted to do more than share his environmental values with her…he wanted to share his bed… *Fold her to me, hold her in my arms, embrace and caress her…*

He felt frustration mingle with desire. She was so set on rejecting him—rejecting all men!

But then, he reasoned, if the kind of men she came across

were all of the same stamp as Karl Reiner, was that so surprising? Rafael's thoughts darkened. And if men like Karl Reiner were used to models sleeping their way into lucrative contracts, exploiting their beauty with rich and influential men to further their careers, no wonder Celeste did not want to run the slightest risk of being tainted by embarking on any kind of relationship with anyone who could be considered in that light.

Such as himself, Rafael acknowledged. His wealth, as he knew only too well, made him a target for just such women, and he also knew that it was precisely the fact that Madeline had already made her own money—huge amounts of it!—that had been a key factor in their relationship. There had been no question that Madeline had wanted him only in order to further her career!

But he didn't want to think about Madeline—he wanted to think about Celeste—

Is she worrying that people might think she turned down Reiner for a man even richer? Is that the reason for her reluctance? Because it would show her to be no better than that other model who did have an affair with Reiner to advance her career?

If so, it was a tribute to her character, demonstrating yet again how right he was to want her as deeply as he did! He could be confident that he could trust her not to be venal or corrupt—not to be the kind of woman who would trade herself for financial advantage!

His eyes shadowed. In his country of birth, still teeming with impoverished masses, there were women so abjectly poor they had no choice but to sell their bodies simply to survive. But here in the rich Western world there was seldom such desperate need. Here it would simply be a matter of making easy money...

In his head, the harsh sound of mocking laughter echoed viciously...

His mouth tightened to a whipped line and forcibly he

wiped his mind of all such tainted, toxic thoughts. Celeste was nothing like that—*nothing!* That was all he had to know. All he needed to know.

Apart from the most important thing of all—how to win her. How to allay her reluctance and wariness and get her, little by precious little, to relax with him. To enjoy his company as he was enjoying having hers this evening.

He put aside such troubling thoughts, focussing instead on making this a pleasant, easy meal to share together, without stress or strain.

He nodded at her with a slight smile. 'Sole OK?' he checked as they began to eat.

'Beautiful,' she assured him.

'And I can't tempt you to a modest spoonful of hollandaise sauce?' He indicated the silver jug containing the butter-rich sauce that went with his own salmon.

'You can tempt me,' she said lightly, 'but I won't succumb.'

Even as she spoke she realised it was a *double entendre.*

Long lashes dipped down over his obsidian eyes. 'I shall live in hope,' Rafael murmured, the now familiar humorous glint in his eyes.

She gave a resigned shake of her head even as her lips twitched with unconscious amusement. She was coming to appreciate that this uniquely disturbing man had a beguiling sense of humour that could tease gently—but not threateningly.

He might radiate the sense of powerful self-assurance that sat on many a wealthy man's shoulders, and beneath the hand-tailored suit there might be an innate underlying toughness that came, she suspected, from the struggles he had faced in his life to make himself what he now was, but for all that—perhaps *because* of that!—there was a chivalry about him that could only warrant her respect and her appreciation. She felt warmed by it. His intervention in that horrible, ugly scene with Karl Reiner was proof of that—as was the open contempt he displayed towards the man.

No, she acknowledged, with wrenching self-awareness, Rafael Sanguardo posed one threat to her only: he attracted her—attracted her as no other man had ever done!

That is his threat to me! That! And that is why I cannot—must not!—let myself be beguiled by him! However much I want to be! I am not free to be beguiled by him! I am not free to want him as I do!

It was impossible. Always impossible. Which was why this evening could not be the start of anything—only the end.

And so I must make the most of it! Have it as a good memory for the future. The memory of what might have been but cannot be...

That was all she could have. All she could *ever* have.

She took a breath, made some polite, praising comment about the quality of the food they were eating, and the conversation moved on. It was easy and yet mentally stimulating, too, as well as pleasant and enjoyable—let alone that it quickened her pulse so powerfully, so beguilingly, to talk to Rafael Sanguardo, whatever the subject.

The single glass of crisp white wine she'd allowed herself helped, she knew, and she sipped it carefully as she ate. Quite what they talked about she wasn't aware—only that they ranged over a variety of subjects. Rafael proved a skilful conversationalist, his wry comments infused with glinting humour, and yet when he was serious—as when they talked about his work and his country—she could see a clear sense of commitment and passion about him.

More and more Celeste found herself thinking well of him, even beyond the oh-so-potent physical attraction that so disturbed her senses. *He is an enlightened, upright man, with sound principles and a sense of the responsibility that comes with the kind of wealth he has made for himself—and made for others, too.*

A man she could respect. The little stab of anguish came

again. And a man she could easily, so dangerously easily, start to feel much more for than respect.

But that reaction must be quashed. She must not give in to her silent urge to hold his eyes, to let her own eyes dwell on the strongly planed features of his face that drew her gaze so much, to let herself feel that shimmer of response to his effortlessly compelling masculinity. She must restrict and restrain herself to being cool and composed and letting no emotion well up from the core of her being.

But as they neared the end of their meal Celeste's determined composure was overset by a quite different source. She had just made an interested reply to something Rafael had said about the new eco-friendly beachfront resort in Maragua that he was investing in when her eye was abruptly caught by a couple taking their place at a table at the far end of the room. They were almost concealed by the red velvet drapery—but not enough to stop her recognising, with a sudden tautening of her stomach, that the man was Karl Reiner.

Then another ripple of unpleasant recognition went through her. The woman he was with was Louise, the young model she'd met the day before.

'What is it?' Rafael asked quietly, seeing her expression.

Celeste swallowed. 'Karl Reiner's just turned up with a model I know is only a teenager and is totally new to modelling,' she said tightly.

She looked as if she was going to jump to her feet. Rafael stayed her, loosely cupping her wrist for a moment. 'Do you think she's underage?' he asked, in the same low voice.

Celeste shook her head. 'No, but she's made up to look my age—which she is not. I don't want—' She stopped.

'Just keep an eye on her,' Rafael advised. 'Has Karl Reiner seen you?'

'No, and now he's out of my vision—he's hidden behind that drape.'

'Well, he's not the important one—she is.'

They resumed eating and conversation returned, but

Celeste was constantly aware of Louise on the far side of the room.

As the waiter cleared their plates and she glanced again towards Louise she frowned. The expression on Louise's face had changed. She was looking vacant, and there was a slackness about her posture. She lifted the glass at her setting and drank from it. Water? thought Celeste. Or vodka? Then, as Louise bent her head to fork her food in a suspiciously slow-motion way, Celeste saw Karl Reiner's hand extend from behind the drape and drop something into Louise's glass.

She was on her feet in a second. Crossing the restaurant in moments. Standing in front of Louise.

'Hello, Louise,' she said. She kept her voice friendly.

Louise lifted her drooping head and smiled. 'Hi!' she slurred. Her eyes were glassy, but at least she'd recognised her, Celeste noted.

'What the hell are *you* doing here?' Karl Reiner leant forward belligerently.

Celeste's eyes lasered him. 'You've put something in Louise's drink. I saw you! And, looking at the state of her, it's not the first time this evening!'

Karl's face darkened. 'You make accusations like that and I'll see you in court!' he attacked belligerently.

A voice behind her spoke. Cool, but with an edge to it that cut like a blade. 'One moment—'

Rafael's hand cupped Celeste's tensed shoulder and he reached forward to pick up Louise's glass. It looked clear and pristine, but he raised it to his nose.

'Roofies don't smell and they don't taste—and they dissolve instantly!' Celeste ground out.

'There's no damn roofies in that!' Karl snarled angrily.

The bladed voice came again. 'Well, if there's nothing spiked about Louise's drink you won't object to drinking it yourself, will you?'

Wordlessly he held it out to Karl. Who did not take

it. It was all Celeste needed. She went round to Louise's banquette.

'Time to go home,' she said bracingly, and helped her to her feet.

'I'm fine,' said Louise, but as she tried to stand up she started to sway, and collapsed back down again.

The *maître d'* was there, having realised something untoward was going on.

Rafael turned to him. 'Bring a small, unopened bottle of mineral water,' he ordered. 'Mr Reiner's guest is feeling unwell, so we'll be seeing her home.'

As the *maître d'* clicked his fingers to a minion, who scurried up with the requisite bottle, Rafael turned back to Karl Reiner.

'We'll get this analysed, shall we?' he said. He took the bottle, emptied the water it contained into the jug on the table and carefully poured the contents of Louise's glass into the now empty bottle, screwing on the lid and putting the bottle in his jacket pocket.

'You can't do this!' Karl pushed to his feet.

'I just have,' said Rafael. 'Would you like me to call the police as well?'

The *maître d'* looked aghast, and Rafael relented.

He turned back to Celeste. 'Can she walk, do you think?'

Celeste drew Louise to her feet again. 'Come on, Louise—let's go.'

Carefully, they escorted her from the dining room. Rafael phoned for his car. As they passed the reception desk Rafael paused to instruct that his bill be sent to his office.

'Oh, and cancel Mr Reiner's room for the night,' he added. 'He won't be needing it after all.'

The expression on the receptionist's face told him that his assumption had been right.

'The upper floors are bedrooms,' Rafael elucidated to Celeste as he guided both her and the woozy Louise out to the pavement. 'And, no, I was *not* planning on availing myself of the hotel facility here tonight!' he added stringently. 'I leave that kind of crassness to the likes of Louise's druggist!'

He got them both into the car and helped Celeste strap in a supine Louise. Then, after Celeste's protracted extraction of Louise's address from her, he instructed his driver and the car moved off.

He turned back to Celeste. 'Did you definitely see him spike her drink?'

'*Yes!* And that analysis will prove positive!' she bit out vehemently.

He held up a hand. 'Celeste, I don't know the exact legal status of Rohypnol, or anything else it might be, but proving that you saw him do it, plus that it was non-consensual on Louise's part, is going to be very difficult—if not impossible.'

He saw the stormy expression in her eyes in the street lights and went on, 'So let's just get her home, shall we? You can read the Riot Act to her tomorrow. But you know...' His voice changed. 'You have to allow for the fact that she was there of her own free will, and might very well have been perfectly willing to go ahead with whatever it was that Karl Reiner had planned.' He took a breath. 'I know it's not anything you could possibly go along with yourself, but there are women who would.'

Women who would do a lot more...

He saw Celeste's face still. For a moment it was as if he could see the bones beneath her skin. Stark and skeletal. But maybe it was a trick of the strobing street lights.

Louise groaned. 'I feel sick,' she said.

Silently Rafael handed Celeste a clutch of paper tissues from the supply in the car. To his relief they were not needed, and some fifteen minutes later they were in Earls Court, pulling up outside the address Celeste had extracted. They got Louise up the steps, and eventually inside, into the hands of the flatmate who had come down to answer the door.

She stayed to explain, briefly, what had happened, sufficiently reassured by the concern of the flatmate, who seemed sensible and level-headed. 'Probably a roofie,' she said. 'Possibly vodka, too. Get her to phone me tomorrow,' she instructed. 'Celeste Philips—we're at the same agency. I have some ground rules to spell out to her if she's going to survive this modelling game!'

After handing over the woozy Louise, she returned with Rafael to his car. Back in the interior, she closed her eyes. Rafael settled in his seat and looked at her. Her face was tight and stark.

'I'll see you home,' he said quietly.

The car moved off and he found himself looking at her, at her pale, haunting beauty which moved him so. Her eyes stayed closed, her face averted, her taut expression not easing.

His thoughts were troubled. In his head he heard again her voice at the restaurant.

'I don't date,' she'd said. *'I don't date and I don't have relationships. Or romances. Or affairs. Or anything—whatever you want to call them. I just...don't.'*

The bald, blunt words echoed in his mind. Setting his thoughts running.

Had what had so nearly happened to the teenage model tonight happened to Celeste? Was that the explanation for the sad, bleak announcement she'd made? Had she been so badly scared—scarred?—that she'd played safe since then?

Does she see herself in that young, vulnerable girl? Was she once such a girl and there was no one to rescue her in time?

If that were so, no wonder she was now so wary of men!

But resolution seared through him. *Well, I must change that! I must show her that desire can be very, very different from lust! I must show her how desire should be between a man and a woman!*

His eyes rested on her where she sat, so close to him and yet locked in her lonely world, so apart, so separate. He felt emotion coursing through him. Desire—sweet and strong, yet tender, too. He felt his hand lift and almost grazed her silken hair, almost cupped the sculpted turn of her cheek, brushed the tip of his thumb across the alabaster satin of her eyelids...

With an effort he drew back, waited until the car had completed its journey back to Notting Hill and drawn up outside her flat. She opened her eyes as the engine was cut, automatically turning her head towards the kerbside.

Her gaze collided with Rafael's. For a moment her unguarded gaze poured into his. He felt his breath catch. Then, before he could stop himself, he was doing what he'd had to hold himself back from. His hand moved towards her, slid around the nape of her neck. His fingers shaped her jaw, lifting her face to his as he lowered his mouth.

As his lips grazed hers he felt her give a little gasp, almost a tremor. But it was too late. He could not stop himself. He could only give himself to the overriding impulse surging within him to move his mouth to enclose hers, to feel the silken brush of her lips against his, feel her hesitation, her uncertainty.

He wanted to sweep them away! To melt them away until she was soft and molten in his embrace! Willing and ardent!

And just for a moment he felt that melting that he sought from her! Felt her soften, yield, felt her tremulous lips start to part so that he could do what every fibre of his being was urging him to do—taste the sweetness of her honeyed mouth.

Triumph swept through him. Not the triumph of conquest but the triumph of trust bestowed, that she had chosen—*chosen!*—to let him kiss her.

And then she was withdrawing.

Instinctively he wanted to catch her to him again, to coax and persuade her silken lips to open to him again. But with a higher knowledge he knew he must not. He must relinquish her. For if he did not she would be scared away again, and what he had achieved would be lost already.

Yet even as she drew away from him his hand lingered at her cheek and the tips of his fingers threaded into her hair. His eyes poured into hers, lambent in the dim light of the interior of the car. Absently he was glad of the smoked glass between them and the driver, but even so he could not care. The whole world could have witnessed this moment! With his blessing!

For she was holding his ardent gaze, open and transparent, and he was seeing into her eyes, into the depths of her, with nothing between them.

'Celeste…' Her name was on his lips, husky and low, and his fingers stroked at the delicate bones of her cheek.

'Rafael—I…I…' She could say no more.

He did not want her to. 'Hush…' He spoke softly, intimately, to her alone. 'This is my promise to you, Celeste.' His eyes spoke with his voice, his gaze rich and full. 'My promise is that if you give yourself to me I will give myself to you in equal measure. With me all shall be well—I promise you. Whatever scarred you long ago will be undone.' He gave a wry smile, letting his hand fall from her while his eyes still held hers like precious pearls. 'We will take it slowly—as slowly as you need. I promise you.'

He drew back, straightening, holding her gaze for one last moment. Then he was opening the passenger door, stepping out, turning back to take her hand in his and help her out. He made no attempt to kiss her again. He would keep his word—take this as slowly as she needed.

But for all that he knew, with an absolute conviction that coursed through him like a strong, dark current as his eyes rested on her with a last, caressing glance, that 'slowly' did not mean that in the end they would not reach the destination that he sought…

Celeste in his arms…his embrace…his bed…

CHAPTER SIX

IN A DAZE, Celeste walked upstairs to her flat. Her mind was reeling, her senses were reeling and the blood in her veins seemed to be alive with a spirit she could not quench or quell.

He had kissed her! Rafael had kissed her! And the touch of his lips was seared upon her own as if he were kissing her still—as if that coaxing, seductive velvet were still working its magic upon her.

Unconsciously she put her fingertips to her lips as she stepped inside her flat, leaning back breathless against the door, her vision blinking in the bright light, seeing not this light but the dim lamplight of the car's interior, the sculpted outline of Rafael's strong face, the dark light of his eyes as they held hers.

Her breath caught. How long—how emptily, achingly long?—had it been since she had been kissed? Years upon empty years!

And never, *never* like that!

No one could create that touch—that softness, that magic!

Only Rafael. Only him—

She pressed a hand to her breast. Beneath her ribs her heart was beating fast, not just from the stairs but from the hectic pulse in her throat.

I should have stopped him! I should have said no. I can't do this—I must not!

But even as she adjured herself she knew it would have

been impossible to have stopped him! Impossible to have resisted the velvet caress of his fingertips, his mouth. Impossible to resist the magic he had woven on her lips.

As if he'd broken a spell...

Freeing her from a prison that had held her for too long.

She gave a little cry. Half anguish, half disbelief. Lurching forward, she hurried into the kitchen, busied herself deliberately with filling the kettle, setting it to boil. Tea—that was what she needed! Tea—strong and hot and comforting and *normal*—that would scald away the last remnants of his touch upon her lips. Because scald it away she must—of course she must.

She closed her eyes. A great anguish filled her.

What he wanted she could not give.

And what she wanted she could not take.

Barred for ever...

Bleakly she made her tea, disposing of the teabag, rinsing the sink out with the remainder of the boiling water, scouring it as if she were scouring her skin, killing his touch.

It didn't matter—it didn't matter that he'd kissed her. How could it? It changed nothing...nothing at all. What she felt, what she wanted...longed for...did not matter.

With unseeing eyes she started to sip the scalding hot tea, sip after sip. Obliterating the taste of his mouth from hers. While, inside her, her heart ached with an unbearable anguish for what must not be—could not be.

Celeste was asleep and dreaming. Despite her fears that it would not, sleep had come immediately after she'd gone to bed, barely staying up long enough to take her make-up off before pulling her nightdress on and slipping under her duvet. She was asleep almost before her head hit the pillow.

And then she started to dream.

But not about Rafael's kiss.

Hands—hands all over her. And she could not stop them. There was a voice, too, talking at her, and she had to hear it, could not block her ears. She could feel her dress falling off and she could not stop it. And then the touching started... the stroking...and the hot breath on her skin. And she could not stop that either.

She could not stop anything.

And there was one more thing she could not stop.

She could not stop remembering.

Rafael replaced his phone in its cradle on his desk, a look of grim satisfaction on his face. The conversation he'd just had had been off the record, but it had confirmed that Karl Reiner was not popular even on his own company's board.

Louise was the first teenage model he had plied with what a lab analysis of the water Rafael had taken from him last night had confirmed as Rohypnol. Reiner's unsavoury reputation had become a liability, and his fellow directors were going to take action—Karl Reiner was about to be removed from the board and sidelined from the running of the company.

Wanting to pass on the good news, Rafael phoned Celeste. As ever, it went to the answer machine, but he was unfazed by it. He was used to it by now. He kept his tone casual and conversational, with only an underlying trace of concern.

'How are you? Have you heard anything from Louise? Let me know if there's anything I can do on that front. And I have some welcome news about Karl Reiner. Give me a call some time and I'll tell you about it.'

He had no very great expectation that she would do so, and he was not disappointed. Instead, addressed to him at his London office, there arrived a card adorned with a Dutch still life from the National Gallery's collection on which she'd handwritten, 'Thank you for your help the other evening. It was very good of you'.

It was signed simply 'Celeste'.

The glint came to his eyes again. Then he picked up his phone and called her number. Not her landline, her mobile.

She answered it promptly, simply saying, 'Hello?' in a businesslike tone.

'Celeste—I'm glad I've reached you.'

There was a choking sound at the other end. The mordant glint in Rafael's eyes intensified.

'How did you get this number?' Celeste demanded. She did not sound businesslike now. She sounded agitated.

'Louise. She was very helpful.'

'Louise?' Celeste expostulated.

'Yes. I called at her flat yesterday evening, asking how she was. She said you'd talked to her and had been "really sweet" and she said how sorry she was, and how grateful to us both, and how she'll never be such an idiot again. I took ruthless advantage of her gratitude and asked if she had your mobile number.' He paused. 'She was thrilled to give it to me, and said you were "really lovely" and "really friendly" and hoped we'd be "really happy" together.'

There was another choking sound.

He waited for it to subside, then continued smoothly. 'So, in order to fulfil her rose-tinted romantic expectations, I would therefore like to invite you to the theatre one evening. Will you come?'

There was a moment's silence at the other end. Then, 'It's very kind of you, but it isn't possible.'

She spoke with what, Rafael could tell she intended to be, an air of finality.

'Louise will be extremely disappointed,' he replied. 'How will you possibly explain to her that you turned me down? She's played cupid, and this is her reward?'

'If you hadn't conned her into giving you my number she wouldn't know anything about it!' Celeste bit back.

'What's done is done,' Rafael replied, unconcerned. 'What sort of theatre do you like? Drama? Musicals? Opera? Tragedy…comedy…kitchen sink—is that the right expression in English?'

Celeste shut her eyes. 'Please,' she said, 'I explained to

you—I don't do this. I just...*don't*, and you have to accept it. Please. It isn't...personal.'

She had to make herself speak. Her throat was narrowing and it was painful. More painful than it should be.

There was silence for a moment. Then Rafael spoke. The lightly teasing tone was gone. In its place was a quiet resolve. 'I'll give you time, Celeste, all the time you need. But I won't give you for ever. Take care of yourself for now.' Then he rang off.

She stared at the silent phone. Then slowly turned it off.

Her heart seemed to be thumping heavily in her chest.

Rafael kept himself busy. It made passing the time until he could get back in touch with Celeste easier. He wanted to give her the time he knew she needed, and didn't want to spook her by being too pushy about how much he wanted to get to know her more, wanted to woo her.

He habitually worked at a punishing rate, clocking up long hours, but now he upped his schedule, taking in a gruelling round of meetings with his existing companies, and with the prospective recipients of his investments, and with financial institutions that might co-fund them as appropriate. Then he flew to New York and did a similar round, heading back to the UK via Barcelona before arriving in London.

The time away had done nothing to lessen his resolve. In the non-stop schedule of meetings and socialising he'd undertaken, Celeste's image had hung perpetually in his mind. And more than her image. It was as if he could still taste the sweetness of her lips, feel the soft silk of her skin, the delicate structure of her cheekbones and jaw.

When, on the return flight, he chanced to be sitting next to a female passenger perusing a fashion magazine, his eyes dropped to one of the adverts for Blonde Visage. Celeste—in all her pale, pure, ethereal beauty! His breath caught and stilled, his eyes devouring her.

How hauntingly beautiful she was! And yet… His eyes shadowed. There was a hauntedness about her, too.

What happened to her in that long-ago trauma that has set her on this isolated course she steers?

Whatever it was—whether or not it was akin to the fate she had saved the young and naive Louise from—he would release her from its haunting! Because the promise of release was there—he had tasted it on her lips, in the sweetness of her mouth.

I can free her from it! I can take her to the place she should be free to go to fulfil the desire that flares between us! I can lead her back from her lonely world, lead her at my side—so she no longer has to be apart, no longer has to keep the world at bay.

Back in London he phoned her, leaving a message on her landline. He heard nothing, and the following morning he tried her mobile number. It went to voicemail. He instructed his PA to send flowers. But at the end of the day she told him the florist had been unable to deliver, and that the occupant of the ground-floor flat had told them she was away.

By noon the next day, courtesy of a call to a harassed-sounding individual at the agency he knew represented Celeste, Rafael knew exactly where she was. Not just away, but abroad. A glamorous shoot on a glamorous tropical island. It had been arranged at short notice, and it was about as far away from England as you could fly.

He leant back in his leather executive chair and stretched his legs under his desk, looking out into the middle distance. Turbulent emotion speared through him. He had thought—hoped!—that his kiss would tell her more than words ever could just what could be between them if only she would let him take her to the place he longed to take her—to the intimacy he knew would light them both. But yet again she had fled from him. Yet again she had disappeared—

He frowned, frustration biting at him. Had she taken

work abroad simply to get away from his attentions? It was likely—and he feared it was so.

Thoughts swirled within him. Should he simply accept, heavily, that what he wanted was impossible? Should he simply relinquish her to the sterile, lonely world she wanted to go on living in? That sad, isolated place she lived her life in—alone and solitary.

But every sentiment within him rebelled at such defeat.

No! I can't let her do it to herself! I can't let her shut out the emotions, the physical joy, that should be hers! If she is haunted by her past I will exorcise it for her! I will rescue her from her isolation...her bleak, sad, self-imposed prison.

And in doing so he knew he would find a joy that only she could give to him.

He sat forward energetically, with renewed vigour. He would not—*could* not—let Celeste languish without making one final attempt to reach her. Convince her that he could bring a joy to her that would free her from her lonely life.

He leant forward, picking up his phone to speak to his PA. Seeking out Celeste one last time would mean a long flight and clearing his diary ruthlessly.

But he would do it.

To win Celeste, Rafael was fast coming to realise, he would do a great deal.

CHAPTER SEVEN

CELESTE CRANED HER neck to look out of the tiny porthole. The plane was banking, bringing into view plunging cliffs lapped by the deep cobalt of the Pacific, vividly contrasting with the verdant green of the island ahead. She felt a little rush of pleasurable anticipation. It was an extravagance, she knew, coming here for a fortnight's holiday to this tiny Hawaiian island after the hectic shoot on Oahu, but she didn't care.

The other models had chosen to stay on at the large, lively Oahu hotel, but Celeste had opted for this small—if fearsomely expensive!—luxury resort on an island so small its airstrip could only take propeller-powered planes. She didn't want nightlife and entertainment and crowds—she wanted peace and quiet and the awe-inspiring beauty of Hawaii.

And when the deluxe SUV delivered her and the other incoming guests to the hotel she knew she had made the right choice. Her breath caught as she walked into the wide, open-air atrium of the low hacienda-style green-roofed hotel. A refreshing fountain tinkled at its stone-tiled centre, and beyond, framed by sprays of vivid crimson bougainvillaea, was a fabulous vista of lush verdant gardens, leading down to the sea beyond. She stood entranced, the delicate blossoms of her welcoming *lei* around her neck, drinking it all in, her eyes alight with wonder and pleasure.

Half an hour later, checked in and unpacked in her room—which might have been the cheapest in the resort but was still absolutely beautiful, with its little balcony overlooking the gardens at the side of the hotel—and having anointed her pale skin with the sunblock that was obviously going to be essential when she was outdoors in daytime, she headed out.

Delight filled Celeste as she walked down towards the beach past the azure freeform swimming pool, through landscaped gardens. Little paths meandered past rivulets and miniature waterfalls, lush with verdure and foliage, and vivid white and pink and red flowers grew everywhere, with sweeping beds of birds of paradise and other exotic blooms she could only guess at. It was hot, but not oppressively so, with a light, fresh breeze off the ocean.

As she arrived at the silken-sanded beach an attendant glided forward to usher her to a parasol-shaded lounger, arranging the towels and headrest for her. Gratefully she settled herself down, accepting his offer of a refreshing fruit juice and iced water. Moments later she was sipping as she gazed, entranced, out over the dark blue ocean, which was lapping the soft sand with gentle waves. A sense of peace enveloped her. She was away from everything else in her life—away from the clatter and noise of London, away from her work, from the frenetic pace of the fashion world.

Away from the man who had intruded into her life even though she didn't want him to.

Into her head leapt his image—as potent and powerful as it always was, as vivid and as real. As disturbing…

And more than just his image.

Like a tactile brush against her mouth, it was as if she could feel the soft, seductive graze of his lips on hers, arousing in her such sweet, tempting sensations that even now she felt her body tremble with the recollection.

Her peace was shattered. She must not let herself think—remember—feel! She must not! She must only remind herself of the impossibility of what he wanted—how it could never, *never* happen!

Abruptly, she picked up the resort's activities guide and

started to peruse it. One activity in particular caught her attention. It was a stargazing expedition to the deserted side of the island—a nature reserve where there was no light pollution from the resort. There would be an astronomer to instruct them, and professional-level telescopes to view the heavens through. Early booking was recommended, owing to its popularity. The cost was high, but it would be worth it, Celeste knew.

As she made the decision to book the expedition she found herself remembering, yet again, how she'd gone out to look at the stars that evening of the charity show at the country house near Oxford. And how Rafael Sanguardo had simply strolled up to her and into her life...

She turned the page decisively. Well, he was out of her life now. And he had to stay that way. It was essential. She could not risk any further contact with him. His impact on her had been too powerful, urging her with every instinct of her being to respond to what she knew he sought from her.

Sadness haunted her eyes. She could not respond—must not respond. However much she might try and forget the past it controlled her still—dictated the terms on which she could now live her life. And that meant she had to abide by what she had told Rafael that evening in the restaurant.

'I don't do relationships...'

The stark, harsh truth was indelible. She had to stick to it—*had* to. And now she was nine thousand miles from him and it must stay that way! But even as she reminded herself of that, another thought slid into her head.

It would have been good to watch the Hawaiian stars together...

She snapped the guide shut. Put her drink back on the table. Got to her feet. She would go for a swim. Change the inside of her head, as it clearly urgently needed to be changed.

Carefully removing her *lei* and her sarong, Celeste stepped over the hot sand and down to the cooling waters of the ocean. She was here to relax, to indulge herself, to rest, to have 'me time' in a fabulously luxurious place.

And that was *all* she was going to do.

And for the next few days that was exactly what she did. She slid into the lazy routine of the resort, keeping to herself except for casual chats with other guests. She drew male eyes, as she always did, but the clientele here were not the kind to plague her with uninvited attentions. Most guests were couples, anyway, either young honeymooners or older couples enjoying a leisured retirement.

Yet although she kept to her customary solitude, sometimes, with a little pang, she felt a flicker of envy as she watched their companionship, their affection to each other, their togetherness…

Then she would look away again. That was not for her and she must accept it.

Must banish, too, the thoughts that followed—thoughts that saw, clearly and disturbingly, the tall, magnetic figure she must not let herself think about. For he had gone from her life now, as she had told him to.

She must be content with what she had. Which, right now, was this magical resort and all it offered.

She'd booked the stargazing expedition and enjoyed the facilities of the spa, had gone out on a courtesy outrigger ride, seen turtles swimming over the reefs and tried a little gentle bodysurfing. Other than that she had done absolutely nothing except laze and swim and pass the days in peace and quiet.

I could stay here for ever, she thought as she lay on her sunbed, half drifting off to sleep in the shaded warmth, soothed by the murmur of the breeze in the palm fronds, the lap of the waves on the sand. Other than that, there was silence all around her.

Until a voice spoke above her. Deep and accented.

'Hello, Celeste.'

She jackknifed to a sitting position, shock—more than shock—jagging through her.

Rafael Sanguardo, clad in a dark blue T-shirt and pale board shorts, reached out a hand to pull an adjacent empty sunbed closer, and lowered his long, lean body down on it.

'Before you ask—because I can see the question...or rather the outraged demand...is on your lips,' he informed her, 'you can blame your booker. I bullied him shamelessly to tell me where your shoot was, and then found your erstwhile colleagues disporting themselves on Oahu. And I must say...' he glanced around '...you have made a wiser choice than they. *This,*' Rafael said appreciatively, 'is fabulous.'

He settled himself back on the sunbed. One of the beach staff came up, having seen a new arrival, and Rafael turned to Celeste, nodding at her empty glass of fruit juice.

'A refill on that?' He didn't wait for an answer, but made his own request, smiling at the young Hawaiian.

When he'd gone, Rafael turned to Celeste again. Emotion kicked in him. It was so *good* to see her again! To be able to let his eyes take in the incredible beauty of her body, her face, to drink it in like the sweetest nectar. The days since he'd last set eyes on her—handing her out of his car after they'd taken the hapless Louise home—had stretched to an endless age. But now he was seeing her again. She was here, so close to him, and it was good—oh, it was good!

She was staring at him. But not with the expression that he was gazing at her with.

'What are you doing here?' she said, her voice staccato with shock.

Dark lashes lowered over darker eyes. Then he spoke, his voice different from the tone he'd used just now. Sombre. Grave. 'This is my last attempt, Celeste. Allow me it—because if I fail now, then you have my word. I will let you be. I will leave you alone.'

Alone in that sad, bleak, empty world you tell me you live in, bereft of all that romance can offer the human spirit—

*denying yourself all that could be yours...all that I could
give to you...*

Her eyes were troubled.

'I thought I was alone,' she heard herself say.

His gaze was level on her. 'As I've promised, we will take
it as slowly as you need.' Rafael's eyes held hers. 'I ask only
that you give me a chance.'

For an endless moment, it seemed to her, his eyes went
on holding hers, asking a question to which she could give
no answer. Had no answer to give.

She knew, with a hollowing of dismay, that the leap in her
heart-rate had nothing to do with shock. And everything to
do with Rafael Sanguardo walking back into her life.

She shut her eyes, willing herself, hopelessly, to banish
his image—the image that had leapt into her retinas, burning with a vividness that was as shocking as recognising
his voice.

'I can't stop you,' she said, her tone low. 'This is a hotel—
if you want to stay here you can. But don't think you can just
take it for granted that I'll—' She stopped.

'Celeste, about you I take nothing for granted, I assure
you,' Rafael said dryly. 'Every step of the way with you is a
minefield. Every moment of communication I achieve with
you makes me feel I deserve a medal!'

His voice had changed again—she could hear it.

'I ask nothing from you except your time and...' he chose
his words carefully '...your trust. Trust me and spend time
with me. You may enjoy it. I'll make no demands on you
other than keeping company with me. Spending easy time—
leisured time—time out from our working lives, our busy
lives. Time to lie here beneath the palm trees, time to enjoy
this wonderfully beautiful place, time to savour the scent of
flowers and the sight of the sea and the sound of the bird-
song. Time,' he finished, 'to gaze up at the night sky filled
with tropical stars.'

He paused.

'Will you give me your trust and spend that time with me?'
She did not answer. Did not accept or refuse.

He let his eyes rest on her a moment. Her features had stilled and she had closed her eyes against him. Letting her silence be her assent.

CHAPTER EIGHT

'WHICH RESTAURANT WOULD you like to dine at?' Rafael's courteous enquiry came as they reached the foot of the steps leading back up into the atrium.

'I don't mind,' Celeste answered.

She was not *in* her right mind, she knew—because how could she be if she was allowing what was happening? What she had allowed to happen all afternoon.

She had allowed Rafael Sanguardo to say those things to her, to settle himself on the sunbed next to her, keeping her company, asking her about the hotel, what she had done so far. She had allowed him to suggest trying the sea together, which she had declined, and so she'd watched him peel off his T-shirt and run lithely down across the hot sand to plunge into the waves, ploughing out through them with a strong forearm stroke before returning to land eventually, dark hair wet like a glossy raven's wing, water droplets glistening off a bared torso that had been every bit as muscled as she'd known it must be, the shoulders just as broad, the back just as sculpted, his thighs just as steely...

She'd been unable to peel her eyes away from his lean, toned body, unable to stop the strange flush of heat that went through her as she had gazed as though the sun had gained an extra fierceness and started beating in her veins...

She'd allowed it all—allowed him to sit beside her on his sunbed, quiveringly aware of his presence, as they'd watched the sun turn to gold as it sank into the cobalt sea…allowed him to help gather her things and scoop up the used towels to drop them into the canvas box by the beach kiosk, to pad with her along the warm stone pathways across the dusky gardens, back towards the hotel.

Allowed him to stand here now and consider which restaurant to take their dinner in.

Together.

And she would allow that, too, she knew, because she didn't want to have to think about this any more. Didn't want to feel the pressure or the temptation to say no, to send him away, to banish him.

She knew, with the strangest feeling inside her, that she didn't want to do anything right now except go on allowing him to be with her.

She also knew, however reluctant she was to admit it, that she didn't want to try and reject that quivering awareness of him, that flush, that rush of heat in her veins that came just at his nearness to her…

'Then I'll choose,' he said. 'Why not meet at the terrace bar in an hour or so?'

He smiled, the lines around his mouth deepening, and watched her go along the pathway that led to her wing of the hotel. He was on the other side of the complex, in one of the cabana-villas that had their own secluded garden areas and their own private plunge pools.

Would he be taking her there one evening? Rafael found himself thinking. Would there be a time when they would not go their separate ways after lazing on the beach, but instead wander, arms entwined, to find a private hour together? The hour between sunset and moonrise…an hour filled with desire and passion and the fulfilment that he longed for—that had brought him here, across two oceans and a continent, to find her…woo her…win her…?

As he set off in his own direction he knew the answer was

still unspoken. However much he hoped for it and sensed that Celeste hoped for it, too.

Yet later, as he walked up to Celeste across the atrium towards the open-air loggia bar, Rafael knew his hopes were soaring higher than ever. She was poised by the balustrade, looking down over the tumbling water feature, and for a second he was back in that Oxfordshire mansion, seeing her at the head of the staircase there, remembering how his eyes had gone to her immediately, how he had taken in a vision of pale beauty, rare grace, and how he'd been struck by how... *alone*...she'd seemed. How apart from the rest of the world.

So beautiful. So alone.

But now she is alone no longer! Now she is with me!

Oh, it was the most tentative of achievements simply for her to accept his company as she was doing, but for all that he knew he had come a long way since that first sighting of her. She was no longer walking away from him, walking out on him, rejecting his overtures, his company. And that, he knew, was an achievement indeed!

But the way ahead—the way he so wanted to guide her towards, for both their sakes—was uncertain, and he had to move with care, with caution. For one rash, rushed move could send her fleeing from him again.

And he did not want that! Did not want it with an intensity that was almost palpable. This was, as he had promised, his very last attempt to win her—and he might lose her yet! Yet now, as he greeted her, he knew that his dominant emotion was pleasure—the pleasure of letting his eyes rest on her, on how lovely she looked, her pale beauty set off by a long, flowing dress in hibiscus-red, floral and graceful. It was gathered at the waist and the bodice was softly clinging, with a wide, low ruffle framing her shoulders. Her fair hair was loose, but drawn back from her face with pearl-edged combs, and her only jewellery was a mother-of-pearl pendant.

He came and stood beside her, not standing too close. He

did not want to crowd her at so tentative a stage of his careful, wary courtship. He looked out, as she was doing, over the lush gardens spreading below the cantilevered terrace, the verdant greenery hardly visible now in the gathering night except where the torches had been lit and at the faintest line of light from the far horizon.

'This really is just exceptionally beautiful,' he breathed, his eyes roaming the vista before him.

Celeste turned. 'Isn't it?' Her cautious, brief smile met his. Admiring the hotel and its grounds was safe. 'I just can't get over how idyllic it is.'

Idyllic it was, Rafael knew, but he also knew, with sombre recognition, that as in every paradise there was a serpent here. The serpent that lay coiled deep within Celeste, engendered by whatever dark trauma had wounded her so long ago, making her feel she had to keep apart...alone.

But as his eyes rested on her he felt the swell of emotion and resolve filled him.

I will draw her to me so that she is no longer apart... alone! So that she can share with me what I so wish there to be between us!

'What can I get you to drink?' His own voice penetrated his thoughts. He welcomed the question. He must keep the atmosphere between them light, easy—companionable. Nothing more than that for now. In order to let her come to feel comfortable with him.

As anticipated, she asked for mineral water, and he went off towards the bar. Behind him, Celeste's eyes followed him. Although the hotel was deluxe, formal dinnerwear was not required, and Rafael was wearing smart but casual trousers and an open-collared light blue shirt, the cuffs turned back. As he came back to her, a drink in either hand, she saw how lean and strong his wrists were, how the natural tan of his skin tone contrasted with the pale brushed cotton of his shirt.

He'd brought a beer for himself, and he sipped it thoughtfully as they stood in a silence that was not, she realised, strained, but which seemed—impossible though it must surely be—natural and easy... They looked out over the darkened gardens, letting the warm night air waft over them. Beyond the gardens the susurrating sound of the waves breaking on the shore was still audible.

As more guests gathered on the terrace, their conversations rising, Rafael turned to Celeste. 'Shall we go and eat?'

She nodded, setting down her glass beside his on the ledge of the balustrade to be cleared away.

'Which restaurant did you choose?' she asked.

'I played safe and went for the fine dining French cuisine one,' he answered. 'I wasn't sure how you were on other styles of cuisine.'

'I haven't been there yet,' she said.

It was the most expensive in the hotel, which was why she'd been avoiding it. A frown furrowed her brow. She would have to make it clear to Rafael that when they ate she would be paying her own share.

They had to walk a little way along a torch-lit pathway across the gardens to the restaurant, which was set apart from the main body of the hotel. The restaurant opened to its own private garden-level terrace, with a view out over the sea beyond the lawn, framed by palm trees. They took their places and perused the menu. Every gourmet item looked tempting to Celeste, and with a sense of sudden freedom she gave her order.

Rafael quirked an eyebrow. 'I suspect the sauce that comes with that has cream in it,' he warned.

'I don't care!' she answered defiantly. 'Every day of my working life I have to calorie-count! But I'm on holiday now—and that includes my diet, too!'

He smiled. 'That's the spirit,' he said. Inside, he felt another spurt of satisfaction.

He took extreme care, throughout the evening, to keep her in that zone. His tone was always light, with humour lurking in his eyes, a smile at his lips. Using every skill at his command, he strove to draw her out and yet keep the conversation sufficiently impersonal—things any two people together might chat about—so as not to scare her off yet again. He started by talking about the hotel and the amenities of the resort, about which she knew more than him, which made it good for getting her to talk more.

'Do you dive?' he asked at one point.

She shook her head.

'Then perhaps snorkelling would do? Will you come out some time? The hotel will provide the equipment, I know. And,' he went on, 'how are you on the sea? Apparently there's a bay around the headland where dolphins gather— we can take a catamaran to see them.'

Celeste's face lit. 'Oh, yes—I haven't done that yet and I want to!'

'Good.' He smiled. 'What else shall we do?'

Skilfully, he steered the conversation along, and as the courses passed he could see her finding it easier and easier to talk to him. In the same mood of calorific defiance that had made her order fish with a buttery sauce, she did not object when he refilled her wine glass.

By the time the waiter placed their coffee in front of them there was an air about her that he'd never seen—an air that was almost...well, *carefree*. That was the best word Rafael could think of.

Gladness filled him. And a sense of well-being. This was the right thing to have done—to have flown nine thousand miles to find her—to try one last time to persuade her to put behind her the ghosts from the past, to forget whatever it was that men like Karl Reiner had forced upon her. Whatever the ugly episode that had scarred her in the past—perhaps one such as she had saved the young model Louise from—he knew for certain it hadn't been one she had voluntarily engaged in. Others might choose to do so—and now his mind darkened, naming no names, but knowing well who he had in mind!—but not Celeste. Never Celeste!

He lifted his coffee cup, letting his eyes rest on her. His breath caught, as it did every time he looked at her anew. Now, with the night all around them, Celeste's so-beautiful face was underlit by the candles on the table, casting her features into luminous sculpture.

How beautiful she is! How much she moves me!

She picked up her own coffee cup, and as she did so her eyes met his.

Met and held.

Emotion washed through Celeste. Warm, vital…

In the flickering candlelight Rafael's face took on the planes of a dramatic *chiaroscuro.* Her pulse thickened—quickened.

How right it seems to be here now! How right to sit here, with Rafael, in this place, at this time! To gaze at him and let him gaze at me, to feel the warm, strong current flow between us…

The question she so badly wanted to answer shaped itself in her mind yet again.

Could I really do what he so wants me to do? Is it possible? Is it really possible?

Doubt and torment filled her mind. Until Rafael Sanguardo had walked into her life her resolve had been absolute. Romance could never be part of her life! *Never!* But he had overset her resolve, made her question all her bleak assumptions about what was no longer possible for her.

And now, as she gazed across at him, she felt that resolve weaken, that bleak determination erode. Longing swept through her—longing to accept, to take what he was offering to her! To take it with all her being! To give herself to him as she longed so much to do!

Could I give myself to this time, this place, this moment? To this man? Could I truly give myself to him?

That was the question that hung like a dazzling star in the heavens, waiting for the answer that only she could give…

* * *

Celeste could not sleep. She lay tossing and turning in the wide bed in which she'd slept soundly and uninterruptedly all the previous nights. She knew what had made the difference.

Rafael.

The man she desired as no other... With a desire that had leapt in her veins the moment her eyes had lit upon his tall, lean figure suddenly beside her on the beach that afternoon!

A desire that was tempting her to do what she had never done. To defy the past, and claim a present that was everything Rafael Sanguardo held out to her!

She gazed, sleepless, at the slowly turning fan over her head. She had never thought this day would come. Had thought that she would continue alone—must continue alone...always alone! Dragging the past behind her. The past that clung to her like a foul miasma, its tainted tendrils netting her. The past that she could never leave behind her. Never cut herself free from—

But never before had she so longed to be able to do so! To take with open heart and hands what Rafael was offering! To give herself to him fully and freely—

She pushed the bedclothes back, strode to the glass doors that opened to her balcony and slid them open, the mosquito mesh with them. She stepped out into the night, glanced upwards. Stars blazed overhead, burning through the golden floor of heaven. So far away—so far away...

Memory coiled in her head. How she had first gazed up all those years ago, when she was as young—as helpless!—as Louise...gazing up at the blaze of stars in a sky where clouds were unknown. Gazing up across the vast distance between where she'd stood and where the stars dwelt in the lofty, remote reaches of farthest space, freed from the mire of the world so far below them.

She had longed, then, to be drawn upwards into their distant reaches—to be taken up off the earth, far, far away from everything that had been happening to her, everything that had surrounded her there below, dragging her into the sordid mire of the world that she'd been so helplessly, hopelessly trapped in.

Yet now, as she tilted her head upwards and gazed at the jewelled sky, it was not the scintillation of the distant stars that was dominant in her senses but the warm, balmy air, the fragrant scent of the blooms upon the trees wafting towards her, the sound of the sea, the wash of the warm, breaking waves, their airy foam dispersed into the tropical night.

The profusion seemed to play upon her skin, lulling her, slowing her breathing. She felt her gaze slip from the distant stars, rest instead on the outline of palm trees, the pale shimmer of flowers in the gardens beyond her room. The warmth of the night enveloped her, the soft breeze whispering over her skin. And in her head the soft whispering of words was taking shape.

You don't need to gaze up at the stars to find beauty and wonder, or to seek refuge in the heavens. You no longer need to long to escape the earth. This earth—here, now— this scented garden, this dark foliage, these velvet flowers it bears, all lapped by the moon-silvered sea—is good. It has blessings of its own.

And beyond the gardens, in his cabana close to the sea's edge, across the smooth-cropped turf, was Rafael.

She felt her heart give a little lift. Rafael! A man who waited for her—waited for her to bestow upon him what she knew—*knew!*—was in her to bestow! Rafael! A man to whom she could give what she so longed to give. For he would cherish it—cherish her—respect her.

Can I be free to do so? Finally free? Free to leave the past behind?

She felt emotion swell within her.

'We can make ourselves anew.' Into her head came Rafael's voice, talking about how even the solid earth beneath their feet was constantly remaking itself. New land,

new continents...constantly forming, constantly remaking themselves.

Her gaze went out across the garden, glimmering in midnight beauty.

*These very islands are proof of that continual change!
Each one has been formed from the liquid mantle deep beneath the ocean floor, each one formed and shaped and made
anew, moving on, ever westwards, each island newborn—
leaving its past behind them...*

Could she do likewise? If the very earth could change
and leave its past behind could she not do so, too? Could
she, too, be new-made like these emerald Hawaiian jewels?
Finally leaving her past behind her?

Surely I can do so!

And surely that was the answer that she sought—she
could leave her past behind and remake herself for the present that was offering itself to her. Give herself to the man
who, alone of every man she had ever encountered, she
longed to give herself to!

Slowly she returned to bed, shivering slightly in the air-
conditioned cool as she shut the glass doors, slipped back
under the coverlet.

And now, finally, she slept. Content, at last, with the
answer she had found. The answer she had longed for so
much...

CHAPTER NINE

'THERE! THERE THEY ARE!' Rafael's voice rose over the rush of the wind in the huge sail of the catamaran as they clung to the tarpaulin with their hands and bare feet.

'I can't see!' cried Celeste. Then, with a gasp of excitement, she saw them.

A school of bottlenose dolphins, rising and plunging to starboard, leaping one after another, effortlessly keeping abreast of the wind-powered sail craft.

'Oh, they're wonderful!' she exclaimed joyously.

The helmsman grinned and shouted something to Rafael she could not catch, the wind whipping at his words.

'They'll surf our bow wave,' Rafael relayed.

She craned her neck, and sure enough she could see half a dozen dolphins rising and falling through the creaming bow wave and then the wake of the catamaran. Then, suddenly, she gave another cry.

'Rafael! Look—*look,* they're beneath us!'

She gazed down, enraptured, into the space between the twin hulls directly below the tarpaulin, as the dolphins swam beneath them.

'The currents bring the fish in,' the Hawaiian helmsman explained. 'Our wake stirs them up, too, and then the dolphins make the most of them. If you come to this bay in the morning you might be able to swim with them. But beware—they are wild creatures still.'

Rafael shook his head. 'This bay is theirs, not ours. We invade their world far too much.'

They were content with this exhilarating catamaran ride—even though it seemed to Celeste she was clinging to the tarpaulin for dear life.

When the boat tacked she slewed sideways, but Rafael was there, holding her firmly. Safely. Then they came about and he released her. But she could feel the imprint of his grip. Feel, too, the echo of the sense of security it had afforded her.

I can be safe with him—safe in this wonderful, blissful present. Safe from the past.

The words flitted through her mind.

All that morning she had felt different. As different as the stars that shone down on this azure water world of the mighty Pacific, in which the precious islands of the sea glittered like scattered emeralds, born from the ocean floor. How deep the ocean was, she thought, how drowning deep—*but here, with Rafael, I am safe.*

Safe in this bright new world, with Rafael at her side, the past seemed very far away.

When they got back to the little harbour and clambered ashore her legs felt like jelly. Rafael saw her wobble and caught her, his arm going around her waist. And once again Celeste felt his anchoring, felt his strength supporting her. She smiled up at him, her hair wind-tousled, fronding wildly out of the plait she'd woven it into to try and keep it tidy.

'OK now?' he said, and she nodded.

He let her go, turning to thank the helmsman. Then they climbed aboard the electric buggy to drive back up to the hotel.

'A good experience?' Rafael asked.

Celeste grinned, brushing back her unruly hair. 'Wonderful! I'll remember it all my life!'

He gazed, enthralled. Never yet had he seen her with so carefree an expression. He could not take his eyes from her. Only a smothered 'Rafael!' from her made him realise he was steering the buggy at the verge. He straightened it and concentrated on driving.

Back at the hotel, they headed for the pool. Diving into its cool depths was refreshing after the heat of the sun and the salty air at sea, and as Celeste surfaced it was to find Rafael beside her. His sable hair was slicked back off his face; strong, sinewed shoulders broke the surface. Effortlessly, he levered himself out of the pool in a single movement, then held down a hand to Celeste. She took it, feeling his strong fingers close around hers, and with similar effortless ease he lifted her clear. Then, refreshed, they settled back on their loungers.

A server cruised by and Celeste gratefully ordered iced water and coffee.

'No tea?' Rafael queried, echoing her order.

She gave a laugh and made a face. 'This is the USA—they don't do tea that's drinkable by the English! I stick to coffee here!'

'Have you travelled much in the States?' he asked.

She dried her face and started to apply more sunblock after her swim.

'Some,' she said. 'I've done a shoot at the Grand Canyon, which was breathtaking. And one in New Orleans—which is an amazing place. And then New England in the fall—also breathtaking. Plus, of course, I go to New York every year for the fashion shows.'

He nodded. 'I have offices there, but I spend less time there now. I prefer to visit the West Coast when I can. It's quicker to get back to Maragua from there.' He glanced at her again. 'Do you know California?'

Celeste shook her head. 'We stopped over in SF on our way out here, but only at the airport.'

'And what about Hawaii? Have you been here before?'

She gave another quick shake of her head. 'No, this is the first time. And it's as fabulous as its reputation says it is!'

Rafael smiled. 'And does it tempt you to go further across the Pacific? Down to Australia, perhaps?'

It was a casually voiced question, asked in the same friendly conversational tone as before, but as he asked her it was as if a shutter came down over her face. Just as he'd seen happen before, in London, when he'd asked her about how she'd become interested in astronomy.

'No,' he heard her say. The single word was negating and final.

He frowned. What had made her close down like that? 'You'd never care to go there?' he probed carefully.

She looked away, unwilling to meet his eyes. 'Not really,' she answered, making her voice as indifferent as she could. Hurriedly she sought to change the subject. 'Did you manage to get a place on the stargazing trip?' she asked.

He had—he'd made it a priority, knowing how much Celeste was looking forward to it.

The expedition did not disappoint.

With no moon, and no light pollution, the night sky was blazing with stars.

'OK, can anyone tell me what any of these constellations are?' The young astronomer, a postgrad from the University of Hawaii earning some extra money, waved a hand at the sky above them.

Immediately Celeste pointed north. 'The Great Bear and the two pointer stars pointing to Polaris, the Pole Star. Then over there...' She wheeled her arm around and proceeded to identify several more constellations.

'Great!' enthused their guide. 'Want to come and give me a hand?' he teased.

She laughed, shaking her head. 'Sorry!' she said.

'No, don't be! It's great that you're enthusiastic,' he said, and then helped others in the group see what she had indicated.

Rafael spoke over Celeste's shoulder. 'You know the

southern hemisphere constellations, too. Does that mean you've already been in that part of the world?'

But she didn't answer him, and appeared not to have heard him. He found himself frowning again.

She is sensitive about it—why?

Did she have bad memories? Was that it? Had whatever it was that had happened to her to make her withdraw from men, from love and romance, to make her so protective of naive young women like Louise, occurred somewhere like Australia? Was that why she was so evasive?

He felt the questions running through his head as he turned his attention back to the stargazing. Celeste, he could see, was clearly rapt, and he was glad. He wanted her to enjoy things—wanted her to enjoy things with him...

He enjoyed seeing with her the secrets of the heavens revealed to them through the powerful lenses of the telescopes—the stellar nurseries, where stars were born; the twin beacons of a binary system, with their different visual spectra; and, best of all, the galaxies revealed not as the blurry points they looked like from earth, but as populous as the Milky Way, teeming with a billion stars.

'To think that their light reaches us from so very, very far away!' she murmured wonderingly to Rafael as he stood back to let another guest take his place at the telescope.

'And from so very long ago,' he answered. 'Those stars have burnt out millennia ago, yet their light still reaches out to us. Their past becomes our present—'

She did not answer him. A shiver seemed to go through her. Rafael sensed it.

'Cold?' he asked. They were high up, on a terraced viewing platform cut into the side of the extinct volcanic peak that had formed the island long ago, and here the night air was cold, not balmy. They had been handed thick jackets to wear, to keep them warm as they stood under the stars.

Celeste did not answer him. It had not been the cold that had made her shiver. It had been the words he'd said.

'Their past becomes our present—'

They echoed again in her head, changing as they did.

My past became my present...trapping me in my past...

She shook her head. No, she would no longer let the past reach out to her. She would no longer let it isolate her, keep her away from what she knew, with every passing day, she wanted so much!

Rafael—Rafael to hold and be embraced by! Rafael to take her from the past, to set her free into a present that she wanted to embrace wholly and fully! Rafael to cradle her in his strong arms, kiss her with his warm lips...desire her with his body...

And she would let it happen! She would make herself anew—just like the continents and the islands did—leaving their past far, far behind.

She felt Rafael's warm, strong arm come around her shoulder, drawing her close to him against the chill of the starlit night. Her head tilted slightly, resting on his shoulder. His arm tightened around her. She pulled her gaze away from the distant stars and looked up into Rafael's eyes. He was looking down at her. His gaze was warm, and very close. And it glowed with a light that was only in the present, only in the time that was *now.*

By the time they got back to the hotel it was gone midnight. Celeste had drowsed as the SUV snaked its way slowly down the unmade roadway to the metalled coastal road that led back to the resort, and as they disembarked she was yawning.

'Off you go to bed,' Rafael said.

She smiled at him sleepily and headed off across the atrium to her wing of the hotel. Rafael watched her go until she was out of sight, then set off towards his cabana-villa in the other direction. As he walked through the night-scented gardens, with the stars burning above, his mood was strange.

He glanced upwards. He desired her so much, the woman whose name was as celestial as the pale, burning stars above.

But there was more than desire in what he felt—what he sought.

What is happening to me?

The question formed in his head, hanging there like a solitary star in his consciousness. Then he shook it aside and continued on his way.

But it hovered still, and in the morning he woke to its presence. It was with him as he set off on his daily run through the hotel grounds, and sprang stronger as he joined Celeste for breakfast. As it did every time, her beauty hit him. Today she was casually but beautifully dressed, as she always was, in a loosely shaped Grecian-style tunic sundress, her hair simply caught back at the nape of her head with a scarf. She had no make-up on, and her skin, despite her assiduous application of sunblock, had developed the glow of pale honey.

'Hi,' she greeted him. Her voice was warm. Her eyes warmer.

He felt emotion kick in him as he took his place. Desire, yes, and gladness that she was smiling at him—but there was more as well.

What is happening to me? The question hung again in his consciousness.

'Wasn't last night wonderful?' she was saying.

'Stars in your eyes?' He laughed.

'Oh, yes,' she answered. She speared another slice of the pineapple that was her breakfast staple.

'Mmm…' she murmured appreciatively as the incredible rich, ripe sweetness of its juice filled her senses. 'This is the best yet! Every morning I think this is the best Maui Gold pineapple in the entire universe—and then the next morning there's an even better one!'

He laughed, reaching forward with his unfurled linen napkin. There was a tiny drop of pineapple juice on her chin and he dabbed it away. An intimate gesture…

Their eyes met, mingled. Then she pulled hers away.

'What shall we do today?' she asked. There was the slightest hint of heightened colour in her cheeks.

'Your choice,' Rafael said expansively, pouring strong black coffee into his cup.

'After last night I'm feeling lazy,' she admitted.

'Then we'll have a lazy day. In fact, why don't we go the whole hog and indulge in a therapeutic massage? Every morning I run past the open-air massage beds by the edge of the sea and think I should book myself in!'

Celeste's eyes lit. 'Oh, yes—definitely! What a brilliant idea!'

His lashes dipped over his eyes. 'I'm full of good ideas, Celeste,' he said.

She felt heat flush through her and knew that he could see it, too. Knew, too, the truth of what he'd said. Resolve filled her. She would take everything that he was offering her, gladly and fully. No more questioning or torment or doubt or fear.

Rafael had reached out to her as no other man had done, had been able to. She did not know why, knew only that with him the past that chained her seemed so far away…so long ago. As far away as those distant stars that had burnt out long aeons ago.

Whose light no longer reached her.

The oceanside massage proved a wonderful idea, Celeste swiftly discovered. To lie in the sheltering shade of the open-sided cabana as the slow, relaxing, rhythmic kneading of a skilled masseuse worked its magic on her back and shoulders was blissful.

Afterwards they repaired to the oceanside bistro for lunch, taking a table dappled with the shade of fronded palm trees towering overhead. Beyond the ocean lapped the shore in gentle waves.

'Not much to surf on here,' Rafael observed.

'You have to go to the North Shore of the islands, in

winter, to get the big swells coming down from the Arctic,'
Celeste replied. 'That's where all the best breaks are—like
Banzai Pipeline, Jaws and Tunnels.'

Rafael glanced at her. 'You sound very knowledgeable. Is
that from personal experience?' He cocked an eyebrow at her.

She gave a smiling, self-dismissive shake of her head.
'No. I've never done more than bodysurfing.'

Rafael kept his enquiring glance on her. Had it been a
boyfriend, then, in years gone by, from whom she'd learnt
about surfing? Someone from before whatever had traumatised her in her modelling career.

'Surfer boyfriend, then?' he asked laconically.

Like a shutter coming down, her face closed instantly.
Just as it had when Australia had been mentioned.

Frustration bit at him. He had no wish to probe into what
he knew must have been some trauma caused by the likes
of Karl Reiner early in her modelling career, but he wanted
to know a little of the ordinary things about her—did she
have family still? Where had she been raised?—just as he
had told her of his own background, and how he'd won a
scholarship to an Ivy League university that had given him
the opportunity to make his way in the world, and how his
parents had been killed in an earthquake when he'd still been
an undergraduate.

Yet she had told him so little!

But now she answered him. It was done reluctantly, he
could see, because she did not quite meet his eyes as she
spoke, but let them flicker away out to the sea beyond their
table.

'My father,' she answered. 'My father surfed. My mother
used to tell me tales about him when I was growing up.'

Rafael heard the past tense in her speech.

'What happened?' he asked quietly.

She looked at him. She bit her lip, her expression drawn.
'One day there was too rough a sea—'

She broke off. The server was at their table, depositing

their plates in front of them. Rafael could have cursed her, but it was too late. Celeste's expression had changed. The sadness in her eyes was gone. She made an appreciative murmur at the exotic seafood salad, smiling at the server to thank her.

'This looks delicious! Thank you!' she exclaimed.

The server smiled back. 'Enjoy,' she said, and headed off.

They started to eat, but Rafael's mind was racing. So she had lost her father young—how young he couldn't tell, but young enough for her mother to have been the one who had told her about her father's love of surfing. A love that had proved fatal?

Another thought struck him. Was *that* behind her clear reluctance—shown to him twice now—whenever Australia was mentioned? Was it because it had been while surfing in Australia that her father had died? He wanted to ask but felt it would be too intrusive, too inquisitive. Instead he chose another response. One that resonated with his empathy with her.

He looked across at her. 'I'm sorry,' he said quietly. 'It is hard—hideously hard—to lose a parent, whatever our age.' He took a breath. 'I can still remember the day when I heard that my parents had not survived the earthquake that had hit my home village. I was at university, almost a grown man, but I broke down and wept like a child—'

There was a catch in his voice. He could not stop it. Found himself blinking. Then there was the touch of a hand on his wrist. Fleeting, momentary, but there all the same.

'To be so far from them must have made it even harder for you,' Celeste said softly. 'But perhaps...' She chose her words carefully. 'Perhaps you can take a little comfort from knowing how proud they must surely have been of you for gaining entry to such a formidable, elite place of education, and how relieved they must have been to know that you were not caught up in the disaster yourself.'

He nodded, taking another breath. 'Yes, you are right.

And I owe it to them—to their endless encouragement of me
as a child to fulfil their dreams for me, which they worked
so hard to enable me to realise—'

Rafael's eyes rested on her. His parents had dreamed of
a better life for their son—a life free of the endless toil they
had spent their years enduring. But they had dreamed of
something even more important for him, he knew.

*They wanted me to find that special person—the one I
could make my life with, the one I could cherish and care for,
who would cherish me in return, with whom I would have
the grandchildren they never lived to see...*

His eyes drank her in, this beautiful, pale-haired woman
sitting opposite him to whom he was so drawn, whose beauty
was not just in her face, her graceful body, but was also in
her temperament, her sweetness of nature, her sensitivity
and kindness, in the determination he had witnessed when
she had got the hapless Louise out of the ruthless clutches
of Karl Reiner.

Emotion moved within him.

*Is she that one? Is she the one my parents dreamt I would
one day find? Is that why I am drawn to her as I have been
drawn to no other woman?*

Madeline, he thought bitingly, would never have been the
woman his parents would have wanted for him. She would
have half scared them, half repelled them. And, as for Madeline, she would have wanted him to discard them as she had
discarded her own lowly parents.

She had made no secret of the fact that she had bought her
working-class parents a luxury bungalow in Bournemouth,
then never gone near them again. She would have expected
him to do the same—to settle his parents comfortably, then
cut them out of his globetrotting, glitzy life to spend his time
exclusively with her, being a glittering, glamorous golden
couple, living in Manhattan, frequenting only the most fashionable and expensive restaurants, jaunting about the world

in a private plane, entertaining the rich and famous, making more and more and more money...

That's not what I want! Not any more.

Once he had enjoyed that lifestyle, with Madeline at his side. But since they had parted—since she had opened his eyes to what she truly was—his outlook on life had slowly changed. Now he knew with a deep inner resolve that what he wanted was right here in front of him, around him. A beautiful place to be, nature in all its cultivated bounty, and the company of a woman who wanted it, too.

And who wanted him. Wanted him as he wanted her...

Celeste. The only woman in the world he wanted...

His eyes rested on her, met her gaze which had returned to him. He smiled at her and drank her in.

And she smiled back at him...

There was sympathy in her smile, and kindness.

And intimacy.

And promise...

Rafael felt his heart lift—lift and sing.

CHAPTER TEN

CELESTE DRESSED ESPECIALLY carefully that evening. Her body felt wonderful after the massage, and she seemed to have a glow about her. Her eyes looked more luminous to her tonight, her hair more lustrous. She'd left it loose completely, and it cascaded down her back in silken folds, feeling cool and sensuous on her skin. She slipped her dress over her head—layers of gauze-fine cotton in shades of blue...azure and cobalt and deepest turquoise in a haze of colour. It was worn off one shoulder, and fleetingly she remembered that the dress she'd worn that evening at the charity fashion show had been, too.

The first time she'd set eyes on Rafael.

A little tremor of emotion went through her.

I never dreamt then that I would be here, with him—now, like this!

Was it possible? Was it truly possible that she was here with him?

But as she joined him on the terrace for their customary pre-dinner drink she knew it was vividly true. The physical impact of his presence overwhelmed her, and his smile, as he saw her approaching, made her breath catch. He took her hands as she came up to him, stepping back from her to survey her.

He said something in Spanish she could not catch and

smiled down at her again. And though his smile was warm his eyes were warmer still...

Warm with desire...

She felt a little thrill go through her—a shimmer of awareness, of more than awareness. *Intimacy.* She had felt it earlier that day at lunch, when Rafael had told her of his parents just after she had told him about her father, his life cut short so young.

A sense of wonder came over her as she thought about that. She had been so reluctant to say anything at all of herself, even of the distant past and her childhood. The past was dangerous—all of it. Yet somehow she had found it possible to tell him something of her father's life, even if only that brief fragment. Tragedy had struck them both, she realised, losing their parents far too young, and perhaps that realisation was another thread that was drawing her to him.

Drawing her closer and closer yet.

How close?

The question hovered tantalisingly in her mind as they went down to dinner, her hand still loosely held in his.

It felt, she thought, with that little thrill again, the right place for her hand to be...the only place...

This is right—it is the right thing to do. To be here with Rafael. To accept all that has happened, all that will happen...

Certainty filled her. And a sense of peace. Rafael had been right all along. She could remake herself. She could leave the past behind.

She would give herself to what was between them wholly and fully, with no more reluctance or resistance.

The past is gone—there is only the present. The wonderful, magical present that has Rafael in it.

Happiness glowed within her, radiant in its power.

They ate, that evening, once again at the French cuisine restaurant by the shore. They had tried others, but this had proved their favourite. The setting was so spectacular, almost at the sea's edge, and the lights from the hotel were shaded by the palm trees and plants framing the restaurant's terrace.

After they had dined they walked along the pathway that led in the opposite direction from the beach, out onto a little headland beyond, where they paused.

'Look,' said Rafael.

Celeste followed where he was indicating.

A sliver of new moon was rising in the east—a slender crescent of silver. Rafael took her hand, nothing more than that, standing beside her as they stood in silence. His clasp was warm and strong.

She felt his fingers twine between hers. Felt her heart-rate quicken. Felt her head turn towards him. Felt the dark glow of his eyes holding hers. So rich, so full...

For one terrible moment she felt panic rising in her, clutching at her throat...then she felt it fading...fading in the warmth of his lambent gaze.

'Celeste,' he breathed, and then slowly, so very slowly, his mouth came down to hers.

His kiss was as soft as the breeze, as gentle as the caress of the new-risen moon. Moving slowly, sensuously, tenderly over her lips.

Wonder filled her, and as he drew back from her she could only gaze up at him, eyes wide, lips parted.

His free hand lifted to cup the side of her face. 'Will you come to me, Celeste? Will you give yourself to what there could be between us?'

His eyes were searching. His fingers tightened on hers.

He took a breath, speaking with more care than he'd known he possessed. 'I know that this has not been easy for you.' And now his voice changed, became both hesitant and more resolute. 'And I know you have scars on your soul.' He took another breath. 'I know that something bad happened to you a long time ago.'

He made himself go on, for this had to be dealt with—the buried poison in her had to be drawn out at last.

'Perhaps something similar to the fate you saved that *ingé-nue* Louise from. No!' he urged, for he had seen the flinching in her eyes, the pulling away of her hand, which he had to reclasp. 'I say this to you only to show you that I understand, that I wish with all my heart that you could leave all that behind you. I ask nothing—only that you trust me. Trust me to share with you what *should* be between a man and a woman…this precious gift that nature gives us.'

His fingers at her face splayed, spearing gently into her hair, stroking with sensitive tips. She felt warmth dissolve through her, felt the terrible fear that had knifed her at his words fade. Her eyes fluttered, her breath caught.

'This precious gift,' he said again, and now his mouth was dipping to hers.

His kiss was as slow, as careful as before, as tender and as sensuous. But now, as his lips moved over hers, he eased hers apart, deepening his kiss. His hand slid around her skull, shaping it, holding her head. His body stepped forward into her space. She felt a rushing of sensation, felt her eyes close, her free hand wind around his strong, muscled back.

His kiss deepened more.

Wonder filled her. To be held, embraced, kissed like this! By Rafael… Here, on this magic isle, beneath the moon and the stars…

As he released her to gaze down at her, his eyes lambent in the starlight, the moonlight, she felt her heart sing—felt it soar. Wildly, like a bird set free.

For one long moment more he gazed down at her. Seeing in her face all that he had longed to see.

He brushed her lips with tender brevity. 'Come,' he said to her.

And she went with him. Went with him along the winding paths, beside the little waterfalls and fountains, beneath the trees with their glowing white flowers heady with fragrance. Walked hand in hand with him, wordless, for no more needed to be spoken between them. Their bodies would speak now.

He led her inside his cabana-villa, turning on no lights, locking no doors, leading her into the room with the wide, waiting bed.

'How beautiful you are! Celeste...my Celeste!'

It was all he said before his hands reached to her, drew her into his arms, holding her wand-slim body against his. He was kissing her again, tenderly, softly, deeply.

For one last moment she thought she could feel the pain of the past seek to catch at her, to leave its slimy trail across her skin. Then it was gone. Replaced by the healing touch that was in Rafael's lips, in the tender, arousing caresses of his fingertips at the nape of her neck, in the strong, cherishing warmth of his body embracing hers.

A sense of wonder—of freedom—swept through her.

This—*this* was how it should be between a man and a woman! This was where desire and passion met—in tenderness and sweet, sensuous cherishing! Never again would the echo of a foul touch pollute her with its poisoned tendrils...

She was free—finally free of the past that had netted her in its prison of rank and fetid memories.

Rafael had freed her! Set her free with every touch, every caress, every sweet and nectared kiss.

Slowly, sensuously, his hand unfastened her dress, peeled its gauzy layers from her. She wore no bra—she needed none—only a wisp of lace around her hips, soon shed, just as his unnecessary clothing was swiftly shed.

His eyes feasted on her, and then, as he laid her gently, tenderly on the waiting bed, his mouth lowered to her. Her hands reached to him—she let her fingers graze wonderingly along the lean, muscled lines of his torso, fold around his back, outline each sculpted plane and curve. His lips were on her skin, arousing her with each soft and sensuous caress in whorls of sweetest pleasure, whorls that seemed to meld and join, until her whole body was a mesh of sensuous delight.

She could hear a moan in her throat, low and husky, feel a quickening of her pulse, a mounting restlessness in her limbs. Her hands pressed into his body, drawing him closer, wanting him closer, wanting to feel that lean, hard weight against her.

He felt her desire and answered it, covering her body with his, splaying over her as his mouth sought and found hers again. Her tender breasts peaked against his chest, her long legs winding with his. His pace quickened, became more urgent, and it drew from her a matching quickening, a matching urgency of desire that sought fulfilment.

A fulfilment he could feel her straining against him to attain. Fire filled him. With swift urgency his thigh parted hers and he felt her lift against him. His hands meshed in hers, pressing them down upon the pillows as he took her mouth again, seeking and melding even as their bodies sought and melded.

She cried out—he could hear her—and he gentled instantly, fearing to hurt her. But her hips lifted to him, drawing him deeper. Fire flamed between them, burning fiercer and more fiercely, glowing with the white heat of a passion he had never felt before, an intensity that possessed him, possessed him utterly. He felt her body changing beneath his, felt its heat, its molten fusion with his.

He cried out, deep in his throat, and heard an answering cry from her, and then the living flame enveloped them both, consuming them.

It burned away from her all that she had feared for so long. The purifying flame seared through her, through every atom of her body. And as it ebbed she knew with absolute certainty that everything had changed—for ever.

Wonder filled her—and more than wonder. She clung to Rafael, clung to his sweated body, warm and heavy on her. She could feel his heart racing beneath the hard wall of his chest. Feel hers racing, too. His arm folded around her back, hand splayed over her spine.

He kissed her, his breathing heavy, smoothing back her hair with his hand. His eyes poured into hers. He said something to her in Spanish, which she did not understand. His voice was warm, and rich with emotion.

And then his forehead drooped, his body slackened. The arm around her back loosened. She saw his eyelids close, felt her own grow heavy. And even as sleep swept over him, so it did her, too.

Bodies still entwined, still fused, they lay together.

'Ready?'

'Yes!'

'OK, let's go.'

They lowered themselves off the rear platform of the boat into the translucent waters. Adjusting the mouthpieces of their snorkelling gear, they dipped down their heads and started to flap lazily across the surface of the sea, their flippers making their motion almost effortless as they gazed down, entranced, into the ocean beneath them.

She could feel her T-shirt billowing in the water. Wearing it was essential for her pale skin—unlike Rafael, with his natural dark tan. Her gaze wandered from the fish, to him, feasting on his honed, sculpted body, clad only in a pair of hip-hugging swimming shorts.

Emotion speared her. Could she really be here with him, now, in this paradise time together? After all her lonely, solitary years, imprisoned by her past, was it really so simple... so easy?

And yet it was! That was the wonder of it—the miracle. That in his arms she had made herself anew, stepped free of the prison of the past.

So easy—in the end, so miraculously easy...

So easy to be with Rafael, by day and by night, to be with him all the time, separated by nothing—not even the gardens of the hotel. She had moved into his cabana-villa and, whilst she was still insisting on paying her own share for meals and any activities, such as this morning's snorkelling expedition, Rafael had refused to accept any contribution to his accommodation. It was costing him nothing to share it with her, he'd pointed out with irrefutable logic, and on that issue she'd had to concede.

And so she was here—here, as Rafael had said, for as long as they both could be. She, for her part, had emailed her agency, saying she would not be back yet, and Rafael had ruthlessly cleared his diary of anything other than remote interactions that he could conduct, if necessary, from the hotel's business centre.

Because Celeste was his priority. Nothing else. Disbelief still washed over him sometimes, to think that she had finally found the courage to trust him—trust him not just with companionship but with passion and desire. For it had taken courage, he knew that. Whatever it was—that 'something bad' that she had glossed over—it had scarred her badly, poisoned her badly. Kept her in that lonely state she had been in, separated from all that she should have been free to give herself to.

But she'd stepped out of the long shadow the past had cast over her. Taken the hand he'd held out to her, stepped back into life—warm and joyous and passionate. To share it with him.

Share it *all* with him.

All that their time together could give them...

After their snorkelling Rafael could hardly wait to get her back to the cabana. 'Time for a siesta,' he told her, the glint in his eyes also telling her that sleep would not be high on their agenda for a while...

Celeste threw him a teasing glance. 'Aren't we going to have lunch first?'

'No,' he said, and kissed her to prove his point. 'You are all I want to feast on,' he told her, as they gained the cool privacy of the villa and he took her in his impatient arms.

'And I you,' she said huskily, gazing up at him, her eyes full with desire.

The desire that was pouring through her. Desire that was

like *terra incognita*—a land she was exploring with a sense of wonder and release that she had never dreamt possible. A land she had thought barred to her for ever.

After so much fear, with Rafael she found there was *nothing* to fear! Only to embrace and accept and cherish. In this blissful, wondrous present the past had vanished like dark smoke on the wind—the clear, fresh wind that blew off the endless reaches of the vast Pacific here on these emerald isles, these precious jewels set in a cobalt sea.

How simple it had been—how easy! Wonder filled her—and gratitude…boundless gratitude. And desire—oh, rich, rich desire. The passion in her body so long starved now filled her every cell, set her eyes glowing with an ardent flame that fired her with a heat that set her ablaze.

She wound her hand into his hair, pulling his mouth down to hers, her body clinging to his as she kissed him deeply, arousingly.

And he responded. Responded with an urgency that only fuelled her own, that only made her hands fumble in their haste to free them of their clothes, to draw him down with her upon the waiting bed and sate her desire on his strong, sculpted body.

How beautiful that body was! How perfect in its form, its texture and its honed, vital masculinity! She let her hands roam across his muscled torso, knowing every contour, knowing, too, with a delight that enthralled her, just how the touch of his hands, his mouth, the skilfully skimming tips of his fingers, could draw from her sensations she had never dreamt of! And how his surging body could ignite her own, could fuse with hers, melding them as one single flame in which they were consumed.

And afterwards…ah, afterwards she would lie in his loosened embrace, her racing heart slowing, her hands limp on his chest, his hands slackening around her. They would lie together, limbs splayed and tangled, heated and exhausted by passion fulfilled, and she would be cradled against him and know a peace, a happiness, she had never known.

Happiness had set a glow about her, like an inner light within her, thought Rafael, gazing at her now, their heads upon the same pillow. He could see it, rejoice in it. It was there all the time—as they walked through the gardens, as they dined and lunched and breakfasted together, as they lay lazily on the beach or by the pool, even as they glanced at each other as they went out running together in the cool early hours of the newly minted mornings, as they talked and laughed and passed the long, easy days, the clinging, passionate nights.

It was a happiness he felt, too, he knew. Lifting his spirit so that this time with her here seemed to be a time out of the world—a garden of paradise found. But the world, he knew, was waiting beyond the running swell of the seas, and it must reclaim them in the end.

But not permanently. That much he knew. Knew for certain that this time with Celeste had changed him fundamentally.

I want her so much to be the one! To be the woman I want to share my life with! But not the life I know—the one filled with buying and selling and making money and yet more money.

No, he had enough money. His money-making days were over now—now was the time to slow down, take a different tack, move his life into a different orbit. Focus more on his work in his own country, improving the living standards of those he had once been one of.

That life would have Celeste in it—always.

But he had to hasten slowly. To declare himself to Celeste now might yet be too precipitate. She had come so far with him—so far from the prison of her lonely, solitary life—but she needed time. Time with him. Time to accept what he was to her—what she, he knew with every twining of their hands, every shared glance, every moment of companionship and intimacy, was to him. Time to be with him not just on holiday but to become part of his life, and for him to become part of hers.

But, however they arranged their lives together from now on, there were practical things to be attended to. They could not stay here on the island for ever. She probably had work commitments ahead of her, which she would want to honour—and he most certainly had his, which he could no longer postpone.

One above all was looming. One he welcomed. It would see justice achieved for someone who deserved it.

In his head he heard the memory of his own voice remonstrating with Madeline about her latest coup—taking over a struggling luxury brand fashion company but firing its founder. Rafael had argued strongly against such ruthless action.

'You could pay him a royalty—just a small one—or make him an artistic consultant...keep his talent in the company,' he'd suggested.

Madeline had not listened. *'Rafe, the man's a loser! A fool.'* Her voice had been scathing. *'He should have damn well put the design trademarks in a separate company and kept it private—and he should have looked after his cash flow. Not left himself vulnerable. Now he's paying for it.'*

'He's an artist, Madeline, a creative,' Rafael had pointed out. *'Naive, possibly, and not good at business, but you own his designs now, and his brand, and with your marketing and financing skills they'll make you a fortune—you can afford not to hammer him into the ground and take everything he values from him!'*

She'd only looked at him. Her deep-set eyes, which could blaze with scorching sexual desire, make him forget everything but sating himself on her lush, threshing body, had taken on a hard diamond brilliance. Her voice had been as hard as her eyes.

'Sentiment is for losers—and I don't intend to lose, Rafe.

Ever. *I've done whatever it took to get here, and I'll go on doing it to get further still. I always have and I always will!'*

Had that exchange finally opened his eyes to her? Made him realise that despite what they had in common—their shared talent for winning the good things in life, including each other—they were very different people at heart? Madeline's ambition drove her to the exclusion of everything else—all other values were cast aside.

Rafael's eyes steeled. When he had finally discovered just how utterly uncaring Madeline was of anything other than fulfilling her driving ambition for wealth—when he had learnt just what she was prepared to do to achieve those ambitions—it had only finished what had already been dying between them.

And all her scornful derision of his shock and revulsion at her revelations about herself had not been able to revive it! Finally he had seen Madeline without the gloss and allure of the passion that had once burned between them. Seen her for what she was—a woman he could never in a million years consider to be someone he could make his life with.

He would never make that mistake again!

And now his gaze came back to Celeste, nestled against his chest, her beautiful face tender in repose. Emotion welled through him.

With Celeste he was not making a mistake, he knew! With Celeste he was doing the right thing, making the right choice! Her difference from Madeline could not be more absolute!

He felt his heart glow as he gazed at her sleeping figure. Celeste was the woman he wanted in his life—for all his life! And to achieve that he was determined.

The first step was to persuade her to come back with him to New York. He made himself broach the subject later that day over dinner.

'I don't want to leave Hawaii,' he told her, his eyes lambent, 'but I can postpone my return no longer. I have people waiting for me whose enterprises and livelihoods depend on my input and decisions. I cannot, therefore, indulge myself here for ever.'

He took a breath, for he could see by the sudden shadow in her eyes that she was as loath to leave as he was. He reached across the table, taking her hand in his, pressing it closely.

'But that does not mean that we have to part.' He took another breath. 'Come with me to New York, Celeste! Stay with me there!' His voice lowered, became husky, and his eyes poured into hers. 'I want you so much, Celeste. I cannot do without you.'

There was a sudden caution in his eyes that she saw immediately.

'If I am presuming too much, forgive me...' he said.

She felt her heart lift—soar. Her fingers squeezed his. 'Do you mean it? Do you really mean it?' Her voice was a breath of hope in her throat. Her eyes widened with the same emotion.

He lifted her hand to his mouth and kissed it—the age-old gesture of homage and devotion to a woman from a man...a man to whom she knew, without a flicker of doubt, she could entrust herself, a man to hold and to cherish.

'Yes!' he breathed. 'What we have here I do not want to lose!'

'Nor I,' she answered. 'I want only you, Rafael. Only you!'

He kissed her hand again, his lips pressing to her knuckles in the sheer relief of hearing her answer. Then, with an intake of breath, he released her hand, picked up his wine glass and took a mouthful.

'We can be as flexible as you need in respect of your work commitments,' he assured her. 'It might get complicated, but I'm sure we can work something out.'

Celeste smiled back. Her heart was singing. Not to have to part from Rafael, as she had been increasingly dreading she must once this idyll here was over—for him to want her to go with him to New York—to be with him. Be part of his life!

How much he has come to mean to me! I could not bear to leave him.

Emotion welled within her.

'In the meantime,' he went on, his eyes pouring into hers, 'we're going to enjoy our very last days together here. And,' he finished, 'I think we should book our next visit before we leave! Coming back here again is most definitely on the agenda.'

He got to his feet, drawing her with him.

'And now...' He smiled down at her, familiar, intimate, making her heart lift as it always did. 'Let's take a walk along the beach and watch the moon set over the Pacific. And let's make our wish to come back.'

She went with him gladly, at his side—the one and only place she wanted to be...

CHAPTER ELEVEN

NEW YORK WAS…well, New York, thought Celeste. As full-on and non-stop as ever. Rafael had had to plunge into work to catch up with all he'd postponed while they'd been in Hawaii, so Celeste had looked in on the New York branch of her agency and managed to get some short-term work. But her heart was no longer in her career. It was, she knew, with a warm, glowing wonder, with Rafael.

Rafael…who had set her free from her past so that it could never haunt or harm her again! She had made herself anew—the past was finally gone from her life. Now there was only this wonderful present! Being with Rafael, living with him, was all she wanted!

As his backlog cleared they were able to have more time together—either spending relaxed evenings in his apartment on the Upper East Side or going out to quiet, out-of-the-way restaurants. Then one afternoon he phoned her from his office downtown and asked whether she would come to a function with him.

'It's an informal initial launch party for a designer I'm backing—not clothes, but handbags,' he explained. 'He's had a bit of a rough time in the past year or so, but I want that to change now. If you're OK with it I'll have one of his evening bags sent round to you—if you could wear something that will show it off?'

'Of course,' she said at once. 'I'd be glad to.'

She was, too, when the bag was delivered. It was a beautifully made clutch, in vivid royal-blue silk, with an appliqué
swirl of what Celeste suspected were real sapphires. To show
it off to its best she opted for a white dress in silk plissé—
a simple design that would not compete with the exquisite
evening bag.

Rafael was changing into black tie at his office, so she set
off on her own for the small but ferociously elegant boutique
hotel at the edge of Central Park. In the lobby she paused by
the function board to see which room the function was in.

'I take it,' said a voice behind her, 'that you, too, are heading for the Leonardo Suite?'

She half turned. It was a female voice that had spoken,
with an accent that was decidedly English.

'Yes.' She smiled, glancing at the woman who had spoken to her.

Some years older than Celeste, she was not as tall—few
women were—but her looks were as eye-catching as her voluptuous figure, moulded by a vermilion gown that set off her
most striking feature: the rich auburn colouring of her hair.

She looked very faintly familiar. Celeste's brow furrowed
a moment. Actress? Socialite? The wife of someone famous?
But she couldn't place her—and it didn't matter anyway.

The woman was returning her regard, but it was a lot
more comprehensive than Celeste's quick glance. Dark hazel
eyes went to the clutch Celeste was carrying, and narrowed
very slightly.

'May I see?' she asked suddenly, and held her hand out.

Carefully, Celeste handed it over. The woman promptly
turned it around in her hands, and then opened it. 'You don't
mind, do you?' she said, without glancing at Celeste and certainly without expecting her to object. The woman looked
at the discreet label within and then, with a snap, closed the
bag and handed it back to Celeste.

'Interesting,' she said. There was the slightest bite in her voice. Then her expression cleared. 'Shall we go up together, since we're heading in the same direction?'

Celeste could hardly object, and they walked to the lift together.

'It's an effective choice,' the woman said as the elevator doors closed on them. Her glance indicated the white gown Celeste was wearing.

'Thank you,' she said, adding nothing more.

'Is it going to be a theme?' the woman asked.

'I'm sorry?' Celeste looked confused.

'Having all the models dressed in white, each with a different coloured bag. It would be very effective,' the woman said.

Celeste shook her head. 'Yes, I see that. But in fact, no— I'm just a one-off tonight,' she said lightly, with a social smile.

'Really?' the woman replied. 'Sounds like he's missed a trick. Which isn't surprising, of course. Tell me, out of curiosity, what's your fee for an evening like this?'

Again, Celeste looked confused. Then she realised the woman had, perhaps not surprisingly, assumed first that she was a model and second that she'd been hired to carry one of the designer's products.

'Oh, I'm not here professionally,' she said, again keeping her voice light. 'I'm just a guest.'

'Really?' said the woman, her eyes flicking again.

Probably, Celeste thought, because she could see that the necklace she was wearing with the white evening gown was nothing more valuable than freshwater pearls.

Fortunately the elevator opened at that point and they stepped out, seeing the entrance to the function suite just opposite.

'Let's go in together,' said the woman. 'We'll make quite a visual impact side by side, I think.'

Again, it was hard to object, so Celeste let her walk in beside her. They paused by the reception desk. Celeste gave her name, but said nothing more as a tick was put against it. Then the member of staff looked expectantly at the woman at her side.

'Oh, I'm her bodyguard,' said the woman with an insouciant air. Then she hooked her arm into Celeste's and moved forward.

Alarm bells started to ring, very decidedly, in her head. She looked hurriedly around for Rafael. To her relief she saw he was already there, on the far side of the room, in a group of people.

'Do excuse me, please,' she said politely to the auburn-haired woman she now suspected was gatecrashing a private party.

But the woman was already disengaging herself from her arm and striding forward. As she did so people made way for her. Celeste suspected she was the type of woman for whom people always made way. Whoever she was, she was either rich enough to buy a couture gown—and sport some very good rubies with it—or something dodgy was going on.

Whichever it was, she realised that Rafael had seen the woman walking so commandingly up to him. She also realised that the other guests were looking at her and very slightly drawing back. Celeste's antennae started to quiver. There was an air of nervous anticipation being generated. Something was going to happen.

It did. And it was pure theatre.

Rafael was standing stock-still as the woman sailed up to him. Every line of his body showed an immobility that made him look turned to stone.

So, too, did the expression on his face.

Celeste felt a little chill start deep inside her. Slowly she started to walk forward. Then the auburn-haired woman reached Rafael and stopped.

'Rafe, how *good* to see you again!' Her voice carried—a rich, vibrant purr—and its English accent made it distinctively audible.

Celeste watched as the woman leant forward to bestow an air kiss on his cheek, then stand back to look at him. Let him look at her.

Which he did. Celeste could see his eyes flicker very briefly. Then, almost unnoticeably, he nodded, acknowledging the woman's greeting.

'Hello, Madeline,' he said.

She gave a little laugh. 'You couldn't *possibly* think I'd stay away tonight!'

Long lashes dipped over obsidian eyes. 'No, I couldn't think that, Madeline.'

His voice was very dry.

And very cold.

Another laugh came from her—rich and throaty. Then Celeste saw her turn to one of the men in the group Rafael was with. He was slightly built, not tall, and he looked, she realised, as expressionless as Rafael. But in the other man, Celeste could see with disquiet, the lack of expression could not mask the dismay in his eyes—dismay and fear.

'I believe you know Lucien Fevre,' Rafael said. His voice was only dry now, with an edge to it that Celeste recognised—she had heard it before, when he'd spoken to Karl Reiner. 'He's the creative genius that *you*, Madeline—' he gave the slightest slashing smile, without a trace of humour in it '—were too stupid to realise was the core value of the company you bought.'

Celeste halted. Suddenly, with total clarity, she realised who the woman was. Realised that she should have known from the moment she'd heard Rafael call her by her name.

Madeline. Madeline Walters. Self-made multimillionairess and the woman Rafael Sanguardo had once been involved with. Belatedly, into Celeste's head came the thumbnail sketch of him that her fellow model Zoe had given her all that time ago at the charity fashion show...

The rich, carrying tones came again. 'The company, Rafael,' she riposted, 'that is now a global brand, with sales that are twenty times what they were, whose stock price has quadrupled, and whose product range is—'

'Is a travesty of what it once was,' he cut in.

Celeste saw Madeline's head go back.

'They *sell,* Rafael!'

Her voice was not a purr any more. There was a harsh note in it that sounded ugly to Celeste's ears. 'They sell in their thousands—their *tens* of thousands! And with the Chinese market opening up even more they'll sell in their *hundreds* of thousands!'

Without consciously realising it, Celeste felt her feet start forward again. She walked up to the group.

'I think this will sell,' she heard herself saying as she held up the sapphire-studded clutch with a little gesture of display. In the same movement she turned to Lucien Fevre— who was still looking terrified, she realised. '*I'd* buy it,' she said, speaking directly to him but knowing her words could be heard by everyone present—as she'd intended. 'It is, quite simply, one of the most beautiful and exquisitely crafted handbags I've ever been fortunate enough to carry.' She spoke sincerely, for what she said was true.

Lucien Fevre's stricken face broke into a smile, and she could see appreciation for her simple compliment in his face.

'I don't suppose,' Celeste asked him, 'they come in other colours as well, do they?'

Lucien Fevre lifted his hands, turning his attention exclusively to her. 'The spectrum of the rainbow!' he said, with enthusiasm in his accented voice. 'Every hue! But that is just one of my collection—over here...'

He started walking away and Celeste followed him to where he was going, which was to a large silk-swathed table with a lavish display of his designs.

'Here,' he went on, indicating with a flourish, 'I have tried to capture the sea. Look.' He picked up a blue-green clutch, made of silk shot with pale mauve. 'Here is the pearlescence of the ocean—and the ornamentation is nacre, which I have also used for the clasp, with Tahitian pearls to enhance it.'

'It's beautiful!' Celeste breathed.

'And here,' he went on, 'is fire! It is the elements, you see—'

She could see immediately, and listened and looked while the designer went through his designs with her. As he did so he became more animated, the stricken look gone completely.

Until, that was, two figures approached them. One was Rafael, and the other was Madeline Walters. As if a spell had been cast Lucien Fevre froze. But it was Rafael who spoke.

'Go on, Madeline, say it.'

He spoke pleasantly, but Celeste could hear the steel in it. She looked at Madeline Walters's expression. She could not read it. But she could hear what she said very clearly.

'I made a mistake,' she said. Her voice was clipped, and she addressed the designer directly. 'I did not understand the fashion design industry as well as I thought I did. And I...I regret the decision I took.'

'Well done,' said Rafael.

His voice was dry—as dry as the look he bestowed upon Madeline. For a moment Celeste could see her eyes glittering, as if she'd swallowed poison. Then it was gone.

She put her hand out to Rafael, resting it on his sleeve. 'There,' she said, 'may I come off the naughty step now, pretty please?' She spoke humorously, as though the toxic expression on her face had never been, and her glance at Rafael was teasing.

More than teasing, Celeste could see, and the realisation did not chill her—it froze her.

It was inviting.

Words formed in her head. Stark, sharp, and carved into her consciousness.

She wants him back.

* * *

Rafael pulled his bow tie clear, dropping it down on the dresser, and slid the top button of his dress shirt open. He stretched his neck, loosening his muscles, profoundly glad to be back in his apartment. It hadn't been an easy evening...

Madeline's calculatedly dramatic entrance had not come as a complete surprise—she'd taunted him, and he'd half expected she would try something on. Her anger would have driven her to it.

Anger because he had sought out the broke and discarded Lucien Fevre and set him back on his feet again. Even more anger because what Lucien was now producing was even better than his earlier work—work that could have been hers had she not treated him so callously when she'd acquired his debt-ridden company.

But something good had come out of her *coup de théâtre.* He'd got Madeline to apologise to Lucien. It didn't matter that the apology had been insincere, as he knew very well that it had. Madeline made a point of never regretting her past actions.

He knew that better than anyone alive...

For a moment Rafael felt his skin crawl. He moved restlessly, picking up his discarded tie and hooking it inside his closet. From the *en suite* bathroom he could hear the sound of the shower running. His expression changed, lightened. Something even better had come out of the evening than just Madeline's apology to a man she had treated harshly.

Seeing Madeline with Celeste could not have emphasised to him more the complete difference between them! Even if Madeline had not been what she was, he would never, *never* prefer her to Celeste! It was Celeste who drew his eye, Celeste who made his pulse quicken, Celeste whose rare, pale beauty made his breath catch!

How did I ever desire Madeline? How could I ever have thought her anything other than overblown and obvious? How was I ever enthralled by her?

He shook his head, disposing of a comparison that was not needed. Madeline was nothing to him—less than nothing—and Celeste…ah, Celeste was everything!

Even as he thought it he realised the shower had stopped and the bathroom door was opening. She emerged, her hair pinned up on her head and a cotton bathrobe wrapped around her. Even in such unromantic garb she took his breath away!

He went up to her, his expression warm, and kissed her cheek, cupping her elbows with his hands.

'Thank you,' he said, his eyes as warm as his voice.

She looked at him questioningly.

He released her. 'Thank you,' he said, 'for getting through this evening as beautifully as you did. Thank you for behaving with grace and dignity—and kindness.' He looked at her. 'Kindness to Lucien. You saw instantly how unnerved he was, and you stepped in to help him through it.'

'I was glad to,' she said.

He nodded. Then took a breath. 'And thank you, too, Celeste, for something even more.' He paused, looked her in the eye. 'Thank you for coping with Madeline Walters.' He took another breath. 'Although I knew she wasn't going to be pleased with what I've done for Lucien—I'll fill you in on the whole sorry saga later—I hope you will believe that I didn't quite anticipate her showstopper.'

Celeste looked troubled. 'I'm so sorry I enabled her to get in like that—'

'Don't be. If it hadn't been you it would have been someone else. Madeline is unstoppable when she sets her mind to something.'

Celeste's gaze faltered.

And if that something is you, Rafael, is she unstoppable then?

But she did not say it. Could not.

Rafael was shrugging off his tuxedo jacket, followed by his dress shirt. Celeste sat down in front of the vanity unit and busied herself letting down her hair and starting to brush it out. Her thoughts were troubled, uneasy.

Wrapping himself in a black silk knee-length bathrobe, Rafael came up to her.

'Let me,' he said fondly, and took the brush from her. With slow, sensuous strokes he started to brush the long length of her hair.

Her eyes met his in the mirror of the vanity unit. His glowed with a familiar fire.

'You're worried about Madeline, aren't you?' he said. His voice was careful.

Celeste swallowed. 'Should I be?' It was hard to ask, but she had to.

He stopped brushing. 'No,' he said. He resumed his brushing, then a moment later spoke again. His voice was steady—decisive. 'Madeline is the past, Celeste. Yes, we were once an item, but we broke up some time ago, and that, I promise you, is that. Her only emotion when I ended it was anger.'

He paused, then went on. It was vital he make Celeste realise that Madeline was nothing to him now—nothing!

'I see her from time to time in public,' he went on. 'We are civil to each other. But that is all. I know she's had several liaisons since, and probably has one running now. I could not care less about that. I wish her neither ill nor well. I am completely indifferent to her.'

Celeste picked up her comb, then set it down again in a random gesture.

'Do you think she feels the same indifference?' she made herself ask. She tried to keep her voice neutral, as though she were asking a question about something entirely impersonal.

Rafael shrugged. 'I don't care, Celeste. I don't care what Madeline feels or wants or doesn't want. And right now...' He set down the brush and reached for her hand, drawing her to her feet. 'Right now the only thing I care about is taking you to bed.'

His voice was husky, his eyes washing over her, and the intimacy, the familiarity, sent a wave of warmth through her.

He kissed her. A kiss as tenderly arousing as it was sweetly sensuous. Meltingly, Celeste gave herself to it, gave herself to him, to everything he was—everything wonderful and wondrous and precious to her. Rafael! *Her* Rafael.

Her last conscious thought before bliss swept her away in his arms was, *Poor Madeline...poor, poor Madeline, to have lost him!*

Celeste was sitting in a pool of sunlight at the desk in Rafael's study. She was making notes and sketching, with Lucien's sapphire-blue evening bag in front of her. Excitement filled her. This morning—the morning after the Lucien Fevre party—Rafael had talked with her. Asked her to contribute her ideas, based on her long experience in the fashion world, to the advertising and marketing campaign that was being prepared for Lucien's relaunch.

She'd been delighted—thrilled. Now she was jotting down everything she could think of, and making little sketches, to bounce off Rafael when he got back later. Dimly she was aware of the apartment door opening. Rafael must have been able to get away early.

'I'm in your study!' she called out. 'Stealing your printer paper to draw on!'

The office door, ajar, opened fully.

'So,' said a voice behind her, 'when you said "just a guest" to me last night, what you really meant was, "just" Rafael's current squeeze!'

Celeste whipped round. Madeline Walters, looking stunning in a formidably well-cut navy blue business suit, which radiated 'power player' with every centimetre of fabric, was standing in the doorway.

Celeste's expression changed. 'How did you get in?' she asked blankly.

Madeline looked scornfully at her. 'I've kept sets of keys

for *all* Rafael's properties, though I've never made use of any of them till now,' she said. She shifted position. 'So, let's have a proper look at you.'

Dark, dramatically made-up eyes flicked up and down over Celeste, who stood there, recovering her composure. Whatever the hell was going on, she was going to stand her ground.

A slightly satisfied smile played on Madeline's vivid red lips.

'How gratifying,' she said, 'that Rafael consoles himself with women who are the antithesis of me! Even if it *does* mean he has to sleep with a stick insect!'

Celeste could hear the purr in her contralto voice and said nothing. Madeline wandered around the office, glancing around, and then down at the sketches Celeste had been making. She turned back to her. Eyebrows raised.

'My, my—multiple talents! Not just arm candy—or just good in bed, as I assume you must be, because Rafe...' the purr was back again '...is *so* very demanding in that respect!' She glanced again at the sketches. 'Are you going to run with my idea of white dresses to show off all the different colours of the bags?'

'It's a good idea,' agreed Celeste, because it was, and not giving credit where credit was due would be petty.

'Oh, I'm full of good ideas!' snapped Madeline.

She wants to get a rise out of me, thought Celeste. *She's come to check me out—scout out the opposition.*

Well, maybe it was time to provide some opposition...

'Not always,' she said, keeping her voice neutral.

Madeline's eyebrows arched interrogatively. 'Do you mean running off with Lucien Fevre's company but not him? Ancient history.'

Celeste shook her head. 'No,' she said pleasantly. 'The idea you've got that Rafael is available to you again.'

For an instant she knew her comment had hit home. Then Madeline laughed. Rich and full and throaty.

'Rafael is ancient history, too,' she said dismissively. She quirked an eyebrow. 'I thought models like you were always *au fait* with all the celebrity news? Haven't you seen that I'm busy with a senator who's tipped to be the running mate of the next presidential candidate? Mind you…'

Once again Madeline's voice changed, taking on that purring note, but edged with something underneath—something that sent a chill down Celeste's veins just like the one she'd felt when she'd realised last night just who the auburn-haired woman was.

'Between you and me, the venerable senator is a little too…venerable. He might make me the Second Lady in the USA one day, but he is, to put it frankly, too…*restrained*… for my tastes.'

She tilted her head, eyeing Celeste.

'So maybe, yes, it would be fun to have one last session with Rafael—something hot to remember while I'm enduring the missionary position for the millionth time! Not like Rafael,' she said, never taking her eyes off Celeste. 'As you must know by now, Rafael is so very, *very*…enthusiastic when it comes to bedtime!'

Her deep-set eyes flashed as she saw Celeste's reaction to her blatant jibe.

'My God, you've coloured up!'

In an instant, her expression had changed. That flash came again in her eyes, but now it was loaded with a venom that made Celeste's already frozen face freeze more.

'Well, well, well…' said Madeline, biting out each word. '*Now* I know what your appeal is! It's not just that he wanted a skinny whey-faced blonde who doesn't remind him of me. He wanted a nun, too! *Blushing* because I said the wicked word "bedtime"!'

She moved towards her and suddenly, Celeste felt Madeline's hand snake around her neck and stroke down the length of her loose hair.

'Such beautiful hair you've got,' she said, 'like silk…'

Her voice was a caress. Her touch soft.

Yet Celeste felt her skin crawl.

She stepped back. An instinctive movement of recoil.

'Whatever the purpose of your visit, Ms Walters,' she said, forcing herself to a composure she was far from feeling, 'you had better leave now.'

'My thoughts entirely.'

The deep, cold voice from the doorway made both heads turn. Rafael stepped into his study.

'Get out, Madeline,' he said.

He said it with an air of complete indifference, as if she were nothing more than a passing nuisance. Celeste saw her deep-set eyes flash with anger at such dismissal. Then a different expression filled them. She moved towards Rafael, who was standing motionless in the doorway, every line of his body showing tension.

'Why, Rafe, darling, you're looking dreadfully stressed out!' Madeline advanced purringly. 'Why don't you let me give you a massage? You know,' she said huskily, 'just how... *relaxed...*I could always make you with a massage.'

She was baiting him. It was obvious to Celeste. And just as obvious was Rafael's stone-faced lack of reaction. Madeline must have seen it, too, for she tilted her head of fiery auburn hair and found a new line of attack.

'No? Then maybe your lovely blushing nun here would welcome it? She looks very tense to me.' Her eyes moved across to Celeste, who stood as expressionless as if she were walking down a catwalk, then back to Rafael, equally blank-faced. 'So, what do you say, hmm?' she asked tauntingly. 'You could always just sit back and watch if you're too puritan to join us...' She laughed mockingly.

Rafael only stepped back out of the doorway, holding the door open for her pointedly. Madeline's eyes flashed fire again.

'No wonder you're stuck with Little Miss Pure here!' she bit out. 'Tell me, do you just sit chastely side by side, holding hands, and sigh at each other?' Her face twisted. 'God, Rafe, what a bore you are. To think I wasted time on you!'

'Out, Madeline' was all the response she got, in a tone that did not hide its note of impatience.

Celeste saw her snap, her temper flaring openly. Before she could stop her, the other woman had snatched up the blue evening bag from Rafael's desk and was pushing past her to the door.

'I'll take a souvenir with me, I think!' she exclaimed, and then, as she gained the large hallway, she halted and turned back. 'In fact...' She turned, and her eyes were gleaming with an expression of satisfaction. 'I'll even do you a favour— *and* your precious Lucien Fevre! I'll take this bag with me tomorrow night to the state reception at the White House! That should be good enough publicity for you! I might even get the senator to buy me some more of them! I could make the damn things fashionable all across Washington, if you like! Is *that* sufficient atonement?'

Celeste's eyes flew to Rafael. His stone-faced expression was gone.

'Senator?' His eyes pinioned Madeline.

She gave that laugh again, the satisfaction in her eyes blatant. 'You *are* out of touch, aren't you, Rafe? Too busy mooning over your pet nun! Yes,' she said, preeningly, 'Senator Roxburgh and I are most definitely an item now. And, since he's *so* likely to get picked as running mate in the next presidential election, you could, if you ask me nicely, soon be on the Capitol Hill guest list. I'll be the Second Lady in the land.'

She turned to go again, having shot her bow and saved her pride, Celeste could see. But Rafael's voice stayed her.

'Are you serious, Madeline?' His voice was different.

She whirled round, animation in her face. She was delighted.

'Oh, yes,' she purred. 'And the senator is so very, *very* devoted to me! Widowed, you know... It's so sad. And you know how expensive political campaigning is over here in the States—I'm *so* keen to help him on that front! Once we're married, of course!'

Rafael's hand brushed aside her preening.

'Then you're quite mad,' he said.

There was a bluntness in his voice that made Celeste stare at him. His attention was focussed only and entirely on Madeline.

'You will never,' he said to her, 'get away with it.' He took a step forward. There was an edge audible in his voice as he spoke. 'Madeline, drop him now. While you can.'

She was looking at him. Her face was different now, Celeste could see.

'You don't *really* think,' Madeline said slowly, 'that anything *you* put out about me will look like *anything* other than thwarted jealousy and open malice? You'll make a laughing stock of yourself!'

Rafael's eyes speared her. 'And you, Madeline, will get yourself crucified by the American press!' His expression changed. 'For God's sake, get real! Do you *really* think you won't get found out? If Roxburgh gets selected, the press will go through everything about you—absolutely and totally everything! And once you're on TV and campaigning, memories will be jogged, I promise you! Someone, somewhere, will recognise you, make the connection—and then they will cash in with the biggest political sex scandal they've ever found!'

Madeline had gone white, Celeste could see. White with fury.

'Don't you *dare* threaten me!'

'I'm not threatening you. I'm warning you!' he shot back. 'And if you imagine *I'd* say a word about it you're even more insane. Insane to think I would want to be caught in any sordid backwash!'

Madeline was twisting Lucien's bag in her hands, crushing it with the force of them. Her face working.

'I *will* get what I want—because I always do! I *always* do! Nothing's stopped me in my life—and it won't now! If I want to be Mrs Edward Roxburgh, wife of the next damn Vice President, I *shall!*'

Rafael took a breath. Hard and scissoring. His eyes were like bullets.

'Madeline,' he said, incising each word, 'you might be the world's most...*liberated*...woman, and you might be worth close to a billion dollars now...but you can never, *never* be the wife of the Vice President of the USA. Because there will never be a Vice President whose wife...' he took another breath, then said it '...once worked as a prostitute.'

CHAPTER TWELVE

THERE WAS SILENCE—complete silence. Then into the silence came the sound of the sapphire clutch falling on the floor. Madeline had dropped it.

Rafael watched her turn, slowly, back to the front door. Saw her walk out of it. Saw her walk down the carpeted corridor to the elevators. Then he crossed to the door and closed it quietly. He turned back to Celeste.

She looked like a ghost.

Regret hit him—regret that she had heard what he had just said. Regret flooded through him that she'd had to endure Madeline at all.

He came up to her as she stood, as motionless as a statue. 'I am so, *so* sorry,' he said, looking her in the eyes. 'I am so sorry that you had to be subjected to that—to *any* of that!'

'She's still got keys to this apartment.'

Celeste heard her voice speaking. It didn't seem to be saying the most important thing, but it was saying the thing that seemed to be in her head right now. Keeping out everything else. Everything that *had* to be kept out.

Rafael swore, then simply said, 'The locks will be changed today.' He took another breath, steadying himself. 'I need a drink,' he said. 'And you look like you do, too.'

She didn't answer, just went to pick up the discarded bag, smoothing it out. She put it on a side table and then, since Rafael was looking at her with such concern on his face that it hurt, she nodded. She followed him through into the kitchen. He got out a bottle of malt whisky and downed a shot in one. She ran some water and started to sip it.

'You're in shock,' Rafael said. 'I can see you are. Look, come and sit down. I need to talk to you.'

He ran himself a glass of water as well, and they both went through into the lounge.

Rafael threw himself onto his usual place on the sofa and looked at Celeste. 'Please—sit down before you fall down.'

Carefully she lowered herself down at the other end of the sofa, her fingers curled around the cold water glass. She looked at Rafael. His face was shadowed, but not from the light outside. From the darkness within. Then, abruptly, he started to speak.

'I didn't know,' he said. 'I didn't know all through our affair, our relationship.' His voice hardened. 'And I wish to God I'd never found out. Except,' he said, and now his voice had the dryness of the desert in it, 'that it was Madeline herself who told me.'

He stared ahead for a moment, seeing nothing but the past, then spoke again.

'She'd been drinking, so maybe that made her rash—but then, Madeline always has had a reckless streak in her. It's the one she uses, gambles with, to make her fortunes. And, of course...' his voice changed again '...she doesn't see it as rashness. To her, it's simply no big deal.'

He turned to look at Celeste again.

'It came out of a conversation we were having—just after-dinner chat at her flat, nothing more drastic than that. We were talking about economics and the conditions required for economic growth in general, such as a financial system that can create reliable and relatively low-cost credit, and so on. And, on an individual basis, we talked about capital formation. That,' he explained, 'is the formal name for ac-cumulating sufficient surplus wealth, or capital, to use for investment. We started talking about how we'd both dealt with the problem ourselves. It's à real problem for budding entrepreneurs without pre-existing assets to serve as security for a loan.'

He paused, then went on.

'I said I'd built up my initial investment capital by working through university, living as frugally as I could. Then, when I graduated, I worked eighteen-hour days, non-stop, for over three years, doing the kind of work that paid a premium because it was so noxious or back-breaking or in godawful places...' He paused again, and then went on. 'When I'd finished telling her, Madeline laughed.'

He looked at Celeste.

'She laughed and said that what I'd endured made her glad she was a woman in business. Because she possessed a natural asset that gave her an ROT—Return on Time— that was orders of magnitude greater than anything *I'd* had to do to accumulate my capital for investment.' He took a breath. 'In six months, she boasted, she'd made three times as much as I had in three years of slaving non-stop. And the work, she told me, had been the most enjoyable she'd ever had. She'd even, at one point, considered making it her main line of business. Brothels, as she pointed out, are never loss-makers...'

He took a gulp of water, and then another, and another, draining the glass as though it might wash him out. Then he looked back at Celeste. There was no expression on her face still.

He got to his feet.

'I'm sorry,' he said. 'More sorry than I can say that you ever got touched by any of this! Let alone found out about Madeline!' His face tightened. 'I wish I'd had the damn selfcontrol not to blurt it out in front of you, but it just came right out because she's being so incredibly blind to the risk she's running! What I warned her about is inevitable! When the electioneering starts, and the global TV coverage heats up, some former client or fellow call girl will recognise her—and will sell the story to the media!'

He took a breath, his face grim.

'If she doesn't find a graceful way to break up with Roxburgh I'll have no choice but to warn him myself, for his own sake, because it will finish his career otherwise. I don't want to—God knows I don't!' His eyes hardened. 'Madeline knew perfectly well when she told me about her past that I wouldn't publicise her method of capital formation! But where she miscalculated, of course—' and now his expression changed yet again, becoming for the first time clearer, as if a weight had stopped crushing down on him '—was in thinking that I would share her tolerance towards her method.'

He looked at Celeste again.

'I left her flat that evening—walked out on her. My decision to end our affair, and for that reason…annoyed…her. She did her best to get me back…'

Into his head sprang the image of Madeline, stretched naked and voluptuous on his bed, taunting him not to desire her any more…refusing to accept his rejection of her… of what she had done…what she was…

He spoke again, willing Celeste to believe him. 'I hope with all my heart you can believe that there is no power on earth that could ever, *ever* induce me to tolerate her again! I wouldn't touch Madeline with surgical gloves on!' he spelt out. His voice iced. 'Or any woman like her!'

She could hear the contempt in his voice, the disgust. The total revulsion.

She pulled her eyes away, her gaze going towards the wide windows that opened out to the terrace beyond. She opened her mouth to say something, then stopped.

Rafael's cell phone was ringing. With a curse, he glanced at the number, then answered it.

'No, I haven't forgotten. I'll be there.' He disconnected, reached out a hand to Celeste.

'I am really gutted to do this, but I've got to go,' he told her. 'That was my PA, reminding me I have to be downtown in half an hour. I'd get out of the meeting if I could, but this guy is flying out to SF this evening.'

He bent to drop a kiss on Celeste's head. She was still looking like a ghost, and he hated to leave her like this, but in a way, although the scene with Madeline had been ugly in the extreme, surely it must have convinced her that Madeline Walters was out of his life for ever.

'Are you going to be OK?' he asked, concerned. Celeste nodded, and he spoke reassuringly. 'I'll be back as soon as I can, but it probably won't be till about seven. Let's have a really easy night in—I think we both deserve it!'

He smiled encouragingly, squeezing her nerveless hand again.

'And, please, don't waste another single thought on Madeline. She isn't worth it. She isn't worth anything—no woman like her is.' He glanced at his watch and swore. 'Damn—I have to go.'

He crossed to the door. Looked back at her. Felt emotion pour through him.

Thank God I've got Celeste! Thank God she is in my life—thank God!

How much she meant to him! How very, very much...
I never want to lose her...

Then, tearing himself away, he left the apartment.

Behind him, on the sofa, Celeste went on sitting. Inside, knives with the sharpest blades were slicing her into pieces.

Though his meeting had gone well, Rafael had spent it itching for it to be over. He wanted to get shot of work, shot of his office and back to Celeste. He'd texted her when he'd got downtown—something warm and reassuring—but hadn't heard back. Now, as he finished running through his agenda for the following day, prior to finally getting out of his office to head home, he checked his mobile again.

His head lifted—there was a text from Celeste. He clicked

it open. As he read, his spirits nosedived. He read it twice through, but it was still the same.

She'd texted to tell him that her London agency had phoned and wanted her back urgently for an upcoming job she felt she could not turn down. She was booked on a flight out of JFK and en route to the airport.

Disbelievingly, Rafael stared at the words. Then, as if a blow had fallen, he took the full impact of her message. She was gone. Gone—just like that.

He felt winded, as if he'd been punched.

How could she just pick up and go like that? How *could* she?

Could she still be upset about Madeline, even after he'd assured her that there was nothing more between them— that all he felt for her was revulsion?

Urgency filled him. He had to go after Celeste right away!

I have to go to her—do whatever it takes to convince her that Madeline is nothing to me!

He called her number. He had to speak to her. But her phone went to voicemail. A crippling sense of *déjà vu* hit him.

His calls going to voicemail, answer machine…

Her abrupt disappearing acts…

The punch to his stomach came again.

With a razoring breath, he seized his laptop and minutes later had booked an evening flight to Heathrow, then he headed down to the pavement to his waiting car. 'JFK,' he instructed tersely, and got his phone out again, retrying Celeste's number, then texting her his flight details.

Then, as if the devil were driving him, he sat back, staring out with bottled frustration at the rush-hour traffic jamming the roadways out of Manhattan.

CHAPTER THIRTEEN

THE LOW HUM of the jet engines vibrated through the fuse-lage as Celeste reclined in her seat. Outside the night was dark mid-Atlantic. She was trying not to think, trying not to feel—trying not to be conscious at all. Willing herself to sleep. But sleep would not come.

By the time the plane landed she was living up to its rep-utation as the red-eye. She looked haggard, she knew, and if she really *had* got an assignment she would have needed a ton of make-up to disguise the fact. But she wasn't going to a job—that had been her excuse for leaving New York.

Leaving Rafael.

No—she mustn't think that. Mustn't say it. Mustn't allow it into her head. She must block it totally, completely. Be-cause if she didn't—

Claws tearing at her, talons ripping her, knives slicing her—shredding her to pieces, into bloodied rags of flesh.

She bit her lip, trying to stifle the pain. Forced herself to keep functioning even if she felt as if she was a walking corpse. A corpse coming through Immigration, walking out into the arrivals area. But not in Heathrow, nor any UK air-port. The first plane leaving when she'd got to JFK the af-ternoon before had been for Frankfurt, and that was where she'd landed. And it was just as well. The unanswered—unanswerable—texts piling up on her mobile told her ex-actly what Rafael was doing.

Following her to London.

The pain came again. Pain for herself. Pain for him.

I don't want to do this to him! The cry came from deep within her. *I don't want to do this to him—but I must...I must!*

She knew with a sick dread that she could not flee for ever. Could not hide for ever. At some point, eventually, she would have to go back to London.

Face him.

An ordeal she would have given the world not to have to face. An ordeal she could not face yet.

I need time—just a few days...

A few days to accept what had happened.

To accept that everything between her and Rafael was over...

Rafael was in London. He hadn't moved from his apartment there since the morning he'd arrived. The morning he'd arrived to find that Celeste had not gone to her flat. Had not gone to her agency. That her agency thought she was still in New York. That there was no urgent assignment they'd called her back for. That they had no idea where she was.

So he'd stayed in London. Where else should he go? If she turned up back in New York he would be informed. If she turned up at her London flat he would be informed. If she contacted her agency he would be informed. He'd even contacted Louise and asked...*begged*...her to tell him if she heard any news about her. He knew of no one else in the modelling world she might know.

But for five endless days now she had simply disappeared off the planet.

He'd stopped phoning, stopped texting. She wasn't going to reply, it was clear. He could only wait until she reappeared out of the thin air she'd vanished into.

He reached sightlessly for the whisky bottle on the table beside the sofa, then stopped himself. He had to get a grip.

Had to control himself. Getting mindlessly drunk to numb himself would serve no purpose.

He set the bottle back with a clunk on the table. As he did so, his mobile suddenly buzzed into life. He fell on it like a drowning man.

'Ms Philips has just returned to her apartment,' said the operative set to watch her flat.

Rafael could feel relief flooding him. Drowning his senses. Gratitude poured through him. He was out of his apartment moments later, flinging himself into his waiting car, and within twenty minutes he was outside her flat in Notting Hill. Launching himself up the steps from the pavement, he pressed the buzzer to her flat.

How long would it take her to answer? Perhaps she was in the bathroom, the kitchen—somewhere it might delay her picking up the entry phone. Maybe, of course, she just wasn't going to answer her door at this hour of the night.

He flicked open his mobile, phoned her. But before it connected the front door was buzzed open. He was inside instantly, running up the stairs to her floor. Not caring if his rapid tread disturbed her neighbours. Not caring about anything in the entire universe except seeing her again—being with her again...

Celeste—*his* Celeste...

Always my Celeste!

Because he knew that now. Knew it with every fibre of his being. Knew it with every cell of his body. He could not do without her. Could not live his life without her. She was everything to him—everything!

Had he once truly, actually considered marrying Madeline? Had he ever been that deluded? It was impossible to believe now. Impossible to believe that he had felt anything for her.

Even desire...

But as he circled the stairwell, two steps at a time in his

haste, he pushed Madeline out of his head. Celeste was everything Madeline was not—and was everything to him.

He rounded the last corner of the stairs onto Celeste's landing. She was standing in the open doorway of her apartment. He'd never been there, he realised with a rush of surprise. Well, it was of no account. She wouldn't be needing it any longer.

His arms went around her, enveloping her in a hug. 'My God, where have you *been?*' he asked into her hair. He drew back, holding her shoulders, drinking her in like a man who had been in the desert for five punishing, killing, waterless days.

She was in a dressing gown. Nothing glamorous or stylish—just a plain, light blue, thin wool, ankle-length, waist-tied wrap. Her hair was in a ponytail, her face bare of make-up. But his eyes feasted on her. She was the most beautiful woman in the world. The most wonderful. The most precious...

He guided her inside so he could kiss her properly.

But she backed away from him. 'Rafael, no—'

Her voice was high-pitched, and there was something wrong with it. He looked at her, consternation in his face.

'Are you all right?' Concern was open in his voice. He wanted to put his arms around her again, hold her close.

'Um...' she said.

She was looking deathly pale, he realised suddenly. His expression changed.

'Are you ill?'

The question shot from him, infused with fear. God, was that it—was that why she'd suddenly rushed off? Nothing to do with Madeline at all! Images sprang in his head of her in hospital, having tests, being told nightmare news...

She gave a half shake of her head.

'Thank God!' he exclaimed. He looked around. They were in a tiny hall, and he could see a sitting room beyond, through the open doorway, with the large sash windows—curtained now—that he'd seen from the street below.

He went through into it and she followed numbly. He turned back to her, having taken in an impression of simple decor, soothing and tranquil, a soft, comfortable sofa in grey fabric, and a pale oak dining table and chairs. There was a pale grey carpet, landscape prints on the walls and books stashed in an open-front bookcase against the wall. An old-fashioned Victorian iron fireplace held fat candles on its hearth.

He looked at her. Words fell from him. 'I've been worried out of my mind.'

Two spots of colour started to burn in her cheeks. 'I'm sorry,' she said. 'I'm...sorry.' She paused. 'But I...I had to go...'

'To a non-existent modelling assignment?' His eyebrows rose.

She took a breath. 'No. You know that was just an excuse.'

He looked at her. Every antenna he possessed had gone on high alert.

'So why did you leave?' he asked. He kept his voice steady. He had to know! If it were because of Madeline then he must find a way to convince her that she meant nothing to him now!

Celeste looked away. Then back at him. 'Would you mind if I made myself some tea? It's been a long journey. I've just come back on Eurostar.'

'Eurostar?'

'I flew into Frankfurt,' she said, 'from JFK. And since then I've been...' She fell silent.

I've been trying to find the strength to do what I must do now, and I don't know whether I can, though I know I have to. I have to because you've turned up now, like this, and I'm not ready... I'm just not ready. But I've got to do it because it has to end now...right now. I have to end it...

She moved towards the kitchen that opened off the sitting room. It was compact, and Rafael came and stood in the doorway, making it seem smaller than ever. Making the air in it hard to breathe.

She filled up the kettle. 'Coffee?' she asked, trying to sound normal. 'It's only instant, I'm afraid. I don't have a machine.'

Into her mind's eye leapt the formidably complicated machine in the Manhattan apartment that only he knew how to use. That she would never learn to use now...

She tore her mind away, focussed only on putting the kettle on, getting out the coffee jar, her tea caddy. No China tea tonight—this needed strong Indian...Assam. With a strength to get her through the coming ordeal.

She busied herself with mugs, with tea and coffee and boiling water, milk out of the fridge—milk she'd bought at a late-night convenience store near the station before she'd got a taxi here. Her mind darted inconsequentially, trying to find an escape. An escape from what was going to happen.

But there was no escape. She knew that. Knew it with the certainty of a concrete weight crushing her. Crushing her in to the ground.

Burying her.

Anguish cried within her.

I thought I was free! Free of the past! Free to make myself anew! Free to claim what was being given to me! Free to take Rafael's hand outstretched to me! Free to be with him—to hold him and kiss him and embrace him!

Free to love him...

Because she *had* fallen in love with him. Of course she had. How could she not? Self-knowledge sliced through her, cleaving her in two. She had fallen in love with him somewhere along the way...some time when she had lain in his arms, cherished and safe...

But she hadn't been safe at all.

And she hadn't been free.

'I want you to tell me what's wrong!'

Rafael's voice penetrated her anguish. His accent was pronounced—a sign of the tension he was under—although he was keeping his voice rock-steady. He sat himself down on her sofa, waiting for her to sit beside him.

Her eyes went to him. Her heart leapt. Oh, how good it was to see him again! How good to let her gaze feast on him, to drink in every sculpted plane of his face, every feathered sable shaft of his hair, every lean, honed line of his body! How good it was to see him again...see him here.

I have to make a memory of this moment! I have to imprint his image on the sofa, so that I can always see him there. Always have this moment...only this moment...

She moved restlessly, hands cupping her mug of tea, going not to sit beside him but on the edge of the armchair by the fireplace. She saw his eyes flicker uncertainly as she took her place away from him.

She didn't want to—she wanted to set down her tea, take his coffee from him and then wrap her arms around him as if he were the life raft of her life.

But she could not do that. She could never do that now. She was adrift, alone on an endless sea that was carrying her far, far away on a current that had started long ago, trapped in it for ever...

'Why did you leave?' he asked.

He looked into her face and knew the answer. The answer he hadn't wanted to hear. The answer he'd thought needed no response from him. But it must, or why else would she have done what she had.

'It's because of Madeline, isn't it?' he said. His voice was quiet. Deadly.

Her eyelids dipped over her eyes. 'Yes,' she said.

He looked at her. The fumes from the coffee cup on the low table in front of him rose in a coil. Madeline had thrown *her* coil around them—he had thought he'd broken it, but it must be tightening still around Celeste or else why would she have run from him?

'She said something to you, didn't she?' he said, never taking his eyes from her. 'She dripped some vicious, toxic poison into your ears before I came, and that's why you left.'

That had to be it—it *had* to! But Celeste was shaking her head.

His face worked. 'Then why—in God's name, *why?* Didn't I make it crystal clear to you just why I would never in a thousand years have anything more to do with her? Do you think I would *ever* want anything to do with her—with anyone who's like her?'

He took a shuddering breath. Celeste was looking at him and her face was set.

His expression changed. Slowly, he spoke. 'You think I was too harsh, don't you?'

His words fell into silence.

He spoke again. 'You think I was too harsh, too condemning. Too pitiless—too *puritan!* Despising Madeline for what she did—how she earned her first money!'

He sat back, drawing a breath. Never taking his eyes from her. Then he spoke again.

'Celeste, I come from a country that is poor—with a level of poverty almost unthinkable in the pampered West, in the developed countries of Europe and North America and Australasia. I come from a region where *peones* toiled on the land, barely scraping a living by subsistence farming or working on the landlord's vast *estancias,* where those in the cities lived in shacks and shanty towns. Where children begged in streets with gutters running with sewage, where they slept in doorways at night and stole by day, and inhaled glue to numb their hunger and their fear.'

He looked relentlessly into her eyes.

'And where women, young and old, would sell their bodies for a meal, or for shelter, or to feed their children! *That,* to me, is poverty! *That,* to me, is need and desperation! And if you think—' His voice gritted with intensity, his eyes burning. 'If you think that I would ever, *ever* condemn a woman in those pitiless circumstances from surviving in any way she could, then you have misjudged me utterly!'

He leant forward now, infusing his body with urgency.

'Those women have no choice! Their only choice is prostitution or to go hungry—or to see their children hungry! They are driven to it by desperation!'

His expression changed. Hardened like steel.

'Madeline Walters never experienced anything like that! She was never going to starve in the gutter! Never going to go to bed hungry! She took to prostitution because it was easy money! That's all! She mocked me because I'd worked hard and long for what I'd saved! Mocked me for working non-stop at back-breaking work in bloody awful conditions when she could earn a thousand pounds a night on her back in a luxury hotel room! She *chose* to sell her body for sex! She *wanted* to do it! She wanted to make money fast—any way she could! And she wasn't fussy about how she did it! *That's* why I despise her. Condemn her. And I would condemn *any* woman who made the same choice—chasing easy money by whoring herself out!'

He fell silent. Celeste hadn't moved. Not a muscle. Then, with a little jerk, she lifted her mug to her lips and took a mouthful. The tea was too hot still, and scalded her mouth. But she did not feel the pain.

There was too much in the rest of her body.

Consuming her.

Slowly, she set aside her mug. Slowly, she got to her feet. Slowly, she looked back to Rafael. The time had come. The moment was here. The moment when she destroyed the happiness she had so briefly glimpsed.

I thought I was free to be happy! But I can never be free—never!

The slicing knives cut into her heart—her soul. Because the past had not gone. It had never gone. Could never be gone. It had become the very future that was now rushing in on her, forcing her throat to work, her words to be shaped, her mouth to open and her voice to sound.

Any woman, he had said… He would condemn and despise any woman.

Say it—say what you must! What you cannot keep silent on any longer!

She had thought she could keep silent. Thought she could silence the past—silence all that she had done. But to do so now was impossible.

She made herself speak. Forced herself.

'I have to tell you something,' she said. Her voice was as thin as a reed.

He was looking at her. Such a short distance away, but separated from her by a gulf so large it could never be bridged. Into her mind came a memory—a memory of standing on the lawns at that Oxfordshire mansion, gazing at the Milky Way. Of Rafael coming to her, telling her about the Chinese legend of lovers separated on either side of the galaxy.

It was us all along…those lovers parted by an ocean of stars.

Pain pierced her as the knives in her heart sliced again.

His face had changed expression. There was concern in it again, tenderness. The pain came again.

'I've upset you,' he said, 'and I'm sorry. I know it must be difficult for you—painful, even—to hear about women like Madeline. Women who *choose* to exploit their sexuality as she did! To use it to make money.' His mouth twisted in angry contempt. 'Easy money.'

He took a breath, his eyes holding hers.

'Celeste, I know you've had some trauma in your past. Some ugly experience that traumatised you—made you lock yourself away in a prison of celibacy because of what had been done to you! I've never asked—never probed. But I saw how you reacted to Karl Reiner when he said those foul words to you—and how you reacted to what he was intending for Louise. I've always thought that you must have been through something similar—and that there was no one to save you from it! So I can understand—I truly can—how distressing it must be to you when someone like Madeline flaunts what she's done and makes a calculated decision to use the likes of Karl Reiner for commercial gain. I *know*,' he said, and his voice was resonant, 'that whatever happened to you, you never intended it to happen! You never *chose* it! You are nothing, *nothing* like Madeline!'

A sound came from her. A sound like something breaking. Her face was stretched like brittle plastic over steel mesh beneath. Her eyes seared him to the bone. Her voice tore like talons.

'I am *exactly* like Madeline!'

He surged to his feet. 'You are *nothing* like her! How can you say that? You *saw* how Karl Reiner was getting Louise drunk, drugged—whatever it would take to get her into bed with him without her realising it was happening!'

A hand slashed in front of him. 'I am *not* Louise! Don't think of me as her, or anything like her! I knew *exactly* what I was doing! And I knew *exactly* how much money I was being paid for it!' Her eyes were slitted like a snake's. 'Because fixing a price for sex is the first and most important thing *any* prostitute does!'

He froze. His brain froze. Stopped working completely. He just stood there, immobile.

She was not, though. She was swaying, very slightly, and there was a look on her face that was entirely and totally blank. As though she were no longer inside her body.

Yet her voice was still speaking. He could hear it coming from a long way away. An endless distance.

'So now you know,' she was saying. 'I am exactly like Madeline. I made the same choice as she did. I wanted money—fast. And I did what she did.'

There was silence. An agonising silence that stretched for eternity. Then into the silence Rafael spoke.

'I don't believe you.' His voice was flat. His denial absolute.

She rounded on him. 'Believe it! *Believe* it, Rafael, because that's what it was! Prostitution! Nothing else—just that. Sex for money.'

'No—' There was horror in his voice.

'*Yes!* It was prostitution—exactly that!' Bitterness and self-accusation scored her words. 'Oh, I tried to tell myself it wasn't—but it was! It *was*.' She took a ravaged, heaving breath, making herself remember—making herself tell him what she had to tell him. What he had to know.

Her voice changed. Stretched thin, as if a wire was garrotting her.

'I'd only just started modelling, and there's very little money in it to begin with. It came as a shock, because I'd assumed—like so many other teenagers—that once I'd been scouted I'd be swanning around in luxury like a supermodel from then on. The reality was different.' She paused, swallowed. 'Sometimes we didn't even get paid—not in money, just in clothes from the collection we'd modelled. So I was... short of money.'

Her voice was flat now, with no emotion.

'But money was what I wanted. Badly. So—I made a decision. I found a way to make...easy money.'

She took a breath, like a razor in her throat. Her eyes were dead now—quite, quite dead.

She cast those eyes at Rafael, not seeing him, seeing only the past, seeing the choice she had made, the decision she had taken.

'Have you ever heard of something called "summer brides"?' she asked, her voice as dead and as expressionless as her eyes. She paused, her eyes still resting on Rafael.

Did he shake his head? He didn't know. He knew only that something was gripping his entrails, his heart, like pliers.

She went on in that calm, dead voice. 'They are quite common in the Middle East. In some places local culture bans all sexual contact between men and women outside marriage. So what they do...wealthy men...is buy themselves a bride. A summer bride. Temporary. Just to provide them with what they want.' Her voice was emptied now of all expression. 'They pay her a bride price. Enough to...to compensate her for the fact that the marriage won't last more than a few weeks at the most. That once the man has...finished with her she'll be...discarded.'

She was silent a moment. Her eyes slid past him, looking into a place that was very far away and yet as close to her as the agonising synapses in her memory. Then she went on, in the same expressionless voice.

'I got a modelling assignment out in the Middle East—an oil-rich city in the Gulf, where a new fashion mall was opening. They were doing publicity shots using European girls, especially blondes like me. It was good money for modelling at my level then, but it still wasn't as much as I wanted. So when one of the photographers' assistants asked me if I was interested in earning more money—a lot more—I said yes. He explained to me the custom in that part of the world. Said that as a "summer bride" I could make a lot of money— fast. That as a blonde I'd be at a premium...my bride price would be high.'

She looked at Rafael again, not seeing him, only letting her gaze rest somewhere in the desert that was the place where she was now.

Her voice changed. Twisted in her throat.

'He called it a bride price but I knew what it was. I knew what a summer bride was. I *knew* it. Knew what it would be called here in the West.' And now her eyes did see Rafael's face. Saw every stricken feature. 'Prostitution. What else? What else is it when a girl is given money in exchange for sex with a stranger? I was given money—a lot of money. And I know what that made me.' She paused. Swallowed. 'What it *makes* me...'

She met his eyes, forced herself to do so. They were blank. Blank with shock. With more than shock.

'There are no excuses for me. I wasn't tricked, or forced, or fooled. I knew what I was doing and I did it. Because I wanted to. Just like Madeline I *chose* to make easy money, fast. *Just like Madeline.*'

She closed her eyes a moment. Then opened them again.

'So now you know why I left New York that afternoon. And why what we had is over.'

A shudder seemed to go through her, as if something were shattering deep inside. Her voice changed.

'Rafael, I lied about myself by not telling you. I deceived you. Because I wanted you so, so much, I told myself that I could finally leave it behind me—ignore that it had ever happened—accept from you what I had come to feel I could never accept from a man. A normal, honest relationship! But when you told me about Madeline, how you despised and condemned her for what she did—what she chose to do— then I knew that all my hopes had been lies! I knew...*know*... that I can never escape the past, never put my past behind me! That by hiding it from you I've been lying to you right from the start! And when I saw the revulsion in your face as you told me about Madeline, I knew—' her voice choked '—knew that I could deceive you no longer. I could not look at you and know that you would condemn any woman who made a choice like hers. A woman like Madeline. A woman...' the breath razored her lungs '...like me.'

She paused, shutting her eyes for a moment, then forcing them open again in order to say what she still must.

'So I left. And now,' she said, swallowing, lowering her voice, 'you must leave, too. I am sorry—truly sorry, more sorry than you can ever know—that I have treated you so badly, both in my deception, my silence about what I did, and in the anxiety you have felt these past days, not know- ing where I was.'

He was still standing there, frozen into immobility. She

drew breath and went on. She had to do this right to the bitter, nightmare end.

'I would tell you, Rafael, that my time with you has been the most precious time of my life—I would tell you that, but for you I have destroyed it all by telling you the truth about myself, about what I've done. But it remains true, for all that, and to my dying day, each and every moment of my time with you will be a jewel in my memory.'

Her voice was breaking. *She* was breaking. She could speak no longer.

She saw him start, saw his face work. Then he spoke.

'How old were you?' His voice was stark.

She looked away again, then back at him. 'I was seventeen. Over the age of consent. And I consented to what I did. No one forced me or tricked me!'

'You were little more than a child!' Anger bit in his voice. 'You were shamelessly taken advantage of! You had no idea what you were doing!'

Anger flashed in Celeste's eyes in retaliation. 'Rafael, my age is irrelevant! Of *course* I knew what it was I was doing—I was having sex with a stranger for money! I prostituted myself! And calling myself his "summer bride" didn't stop it being that! I told you—I wanted money fast, a lot of it, and I got it. I got what I wanted! Just like Madeline did!'

'I absolutely refuse to compare you to her!'

'Well, you must! I'm sorry—I'm desperately, desperately sorry to inflict this on you, but—'

He cut across her. 'Are you? *Are* you sorry?' He seized on her words, silencing her.

She looked at him. 'Of *course* I'm sorry for doing this to you—'

He cut across her again. 'But are you sorry for doing this to *you?* Now, with your adult eyes, surely to God you bitterly regret what you did? Because Madeline doesn't! Madeline does not think she did anything at all to regret! But do *you?*

Do you regret it, Celeste? Do you look back now and wish you had not done it? Do you regret what you did?'

Every word was loaded. Every word carried a weight he could hardly bear. Her answer would tell him everything he had to know.

Everything he had to hope.

She looked at him. Looked at him with eyes that saw his pain.

And then she inflicted more. The killing blow.

She shook her head. 'No,' she said. 'I don't. I don't regret it. It got me what I wanted. Easy money. Fast.' She paused a fraction of a second. 'So you see I am just like Madeline…'

For one long, last moment he looked at her. Into the space between them went everything that he had once held so dear.

Then, without a word, he turned and left.

The night sky was cloudy, with rain threatening. No stars were visible. He walked. He walked without stopping, without pausing. Somewhere behind him his car was trailing him, his driver probably thinking him mad, but he could not think about that now. He could not think about anything.

Least of all about Celeste.

Who was not Celeste at all. Who was not the woman he had seen and sought, whose trust he had so slowly won. The trust to give herself to him knowing he would never hurt her.

Savage pain lacerated him.

I trusted her—trusted her. Believed in her—believed her to be nothing like Madeline…

His face twisted. In his head he heard, over and over again, her voice crying out. *'I am just like Madeline!'*

And inside his head, all the things that Madeline had told him about herself forced their way in, in sickening, vivid detail. His revulsion had been instant—total. And her mockery of him for it had been virulent. She'd been incredulous at his reaction, refusing to believe he was shocked by her revelation. He could hear her voice now, inside his head, scornful and scathing.

'Oh, for God's sake, Rafe, sex workers aren't some kind of "fallen women" any more! Sex is just a commodity—an industry like any other! There's a market for sex and people buy and sell in it! What the hell's wrong with that? I had natural assets to capitalise on and I sold what my customers wanted—and my profit margin was the best I've ever achieved! So don't look down your damn puritan nose at me and quote Victorian morality like you want me whipped in the stocks as a warning to other women!'

He hadn't answered her—hadn't been able to—and his silence only infuriated her more. Her eyes had flashed with anger. Her voice with scorn.

'What's your damn problem? Most men would think it a fantasy come true, what I've told you! Personal, private, on-tap professional sex! Which, I would point out, you've been enjoying with me for quite some time! I didn't hear you complain while we were in bed! But if you think I've got boring, darling, well, let me spice it up for you! Because I can do that—with pleasure. Pleasure and a great deal of experience!'

He still had not spoken to her. Only his expression had shown his reaction. Then he'd turned to go. Her voice had screamed after him.

'Don't you dare walk out on me! Don't you bloody dare! Women don't have to put up with your kind of attitude any more! We are strong, we are independent and we can make our own millions—and we can have sex any damn way we want it, without men like you looking down on us! Half a century of feminism has made us free of men like you and your condemnation!'

He'd stopped then, turned back to look at her. Then he'd spoken to her. His voice flat. Bleak.

'Half a century of feminism and all you've achieved, Madeline, is the oldest profession of all. You debase yourself,

*and you debase sex. It should be a gift, freely given by each
partner, not a commodity to be sold for a cash profit. And if
you cannot see that, if you cannot regret what you did, then
there can be nothing more between us.'*

He'd gone then—walked out of her flat and out of her life.

And now he'd done the same to Celeste. Walked away
from her.

Inside, a voice was protesting. *Not Celeste—not Celeste!
She can't be like that—she can't!*

Not the woman he'd held in his arms night after night. Not
the woman he'd been sharing his life with. A blow landed
on his heart. Not the woman he'd wanted to go on sharing
his life with.

For the bitterest truth of all was that in the anguished days
he'd spent not knowing where she was, one overwhelming
realisation had hit him. He did not want to be without her.
He wanted her to be with him—stay with him. Make her
life with him.

The realisation had shone like a beacon, impossible for
him to deny, impossible for him to do anything other than
reel from the truth of it.

A beacon that she had extinguished with one fatal ut-
terance.

Pain jagged through him.

He walked on into the night.

CHAPTER FOURTEEN

CELESTE SHIVERED AS she stepped out of her front door onto the steps to the pavement. Though she was wearing a warm coat, the winter weather was cold. But it was more than the weather that chilled her. She was cold in her bones. Cold all the way through.

Sometimes, even though she tried desperately—despairingly—to keep them out, memories forced their way into her head, memories of when she had been warm...

The balmy Hawaiian breeze from the ocean, the heat of the day rising up from the hot sand, the sun like a benediction on her.

The memories mocked her. Mocked her just as all her memories mocked her. With cruel, jeering laughter. Mocking her for having dared to think that she could find happiness, that she could escape the past. Walk free of it.

Of course you couldn't! You were a fool to think you could! A fool to think you could just ignore it, blank it out of your consciousness! A fool to think you could set it aside as though it had never happened—as though you'd never done what you did! A fool to think you could allow yourself to have what you knew from the start must be impossible!

Yet you thought you could have it—you thought you could finally take for yourself the happiness that was barred to you. And all you have achieved is to wound a good man—a man who cared for you and cherished you, a man you deceived by your silence. You betrayed his trust in you.

Remorse filled her—remorse at what she had done to Rafael. At her culpable silence, her self-blinding foolish hope that she could take what he offered her—take the happiness she'd found with him.

Telling him the truth had been like stabbing him... And the knife had thrust into her as well. A lethal, deadly thrust to the heart.

And you deserve it! You deserve to feel that pain, to feel it now, still and for ever! You deserve it for what you did to him! You deserve your broken heart.

She had broken it herself. No one to blame but her. No one to rail against but her. No one to mock but her.

She hugged the coat around her, against the bitter arctic wind. There was no spare flesh on her to warm her. She was thinner than ever, for she had no appetite at all. But it was *good* that she was so thin. She'd done the autumn fashion shows, and now she was booked in for the round of shows that would take place before the spring.

She would be as gaunt and starved as even the most demanding designer wanted, she thought mockingly. It would be exhausting, non-stop, but she'd welcome it—just as she had welcomed the punishing pace of the autumn shows. For it would blot out the rest of the world for her. Not that she could do anything but just get through them. Tough them out until they were all over. And then... She took a lungful of freezing air. Then she would quit. Quit everything.

She could not face continuing with her career. Could not face the absurd triviality of fashion, the endless fuss and furore over what was so entirely pointless, so utterly unimportant. Who cared what hemlines and silhouettes and colours and fabrics were in or out? Who cared which designers were on a roll and which in decline? Who cared?

Where once she might have had a careless tolerance now she had none. Only a bleak, chill emptiness.

About everything.

What she would do when she no longer modelled she didn't know. Didn't care. Could not care. She would sell her flat, that much she knew, because she could not bear to be in London any more. Where she would go, though, she didn't know either. Somewhere far away. Remote. A Scottish glen, a Welsh hillside, a Yorkshire moor... It didn't matter where.

Because wherever she went she would be trapped in her past—the past she could never leave behind her. The past that had destroyed her happiness, broken her heart...condemned her to a future of perpetual loneliness.

Loveless and alone.

Without Rafael for ever...

The small podium was illuminated by light, which also pooled on the rainbow-hued display of clutch bags at the side of the man who was speaking.

'But my greatest gratitude,' Lucien Fevre was saying, 'must go to the man who had faith in me and whose generous support has enabled me to bring you this collection today.'

He turned towards Rafael, who was standing some way away, letting Lucien have the limelight. But he smiled and nodded in acknowledgement.

He did not feel like smiling. He never felt like smiling. There was a grimness on his features, and he knew his staff found his manner intimidating. He could not alter it. It was permanent, he knew. A kind of bleakness of the soul.

Lucien was speaking still, moving on to the others he wanted to thank for their support. It was the official launch of his new company, his new collection, and it was going well. The fashion editors and their ilk were praising the collection, welcoming his revival, and since Rafael had ensured that Lucien had a crack management team around him—everything from publicity to finance—all the signs were that this time around he would not hit the rocks as he had before.

He was glad for him—though he wished with grim endurance that he did not have to be here at this moment.

It was too close a reminder of the informal party held for Lucien when Madeline had arrived like the uninvited witch in a fairy tale. And the curse of her presence had borne its baleful fruit. As had his own denunciation of her.

If I'd never warned her about her insanely unachievable political ambitions...! If I'd never thrown in her face just why they were so impossible...! Then Celeste would never have known why I ended it with Madeline...

And if she had never known then she would never have told me about herself. The punishing logic tolled through his head. He felt his stomach clench. And if she hadn't—?

I would have never walked out on her. And she would still be with me.

Pain stabbed at him. He knew what he had lost.

But if she had never told him about herself—never confessed her past to him—then they would have been living a lie...a lie of silence by her. After wrenching Madeline out of his life, as he had made himself do, there had been times when he'd cursed her for telling him about what she had done—just as he was now so torn about Celeste's confession to him.

But what he had felt about Madeline, about ending everything with her, was nothing to what he felt now. How could it be?

For, whatever he had once felt about Madeline, never at any time had he felt anything at all of what he had come to feel for Celeste.

I never fell in love with Madeline...

The words formed and shaped and burned in his head. Burning through his flesh...burning through his heart.

Lucien had finished his speech and the audience was breaking up, the proceedings becoming informal now. Rafael watched Lucien being approached by two influential fashion directors who were smiling enthusiastically. Rafael started to mingle, doing his bit, but a few minutes later Lucien was at his side.

'I was so sorry to find that Celeste was not here,' he said. 'I had hoped she would be.'

Rafael gave a reply that he hoped was not too clipped—something about her working in Europe at the moment.

'I was hoping she would be here,' Lucien went on to say, 'so that she could take her pick from the collection. I wanted to give her whichever she liked best.' He looked at Rafael. 'I will not forget her kindness to me when Madeline Walters gatecrashed. It is so rare to find kindness and beauty together.'

'Yes,' said Rafael, 'it is.'

Saying more than that was not possible. He moved the conversation on—away from the dagger in his heart that was Celeste.

But as more people came up to Lucien, keen to speak to him, and Rafael stepped aside to let them, Lucien's words echoed in his head.

'I will not forget her kindness...'

In his memory he saw the scene again—Celeste going up to Lucien, intervening, diverting him from Madeline's scornful boasts of sales and profit. She'd seen his distress and taken action.

Another memory played inside his head. Just as she'd taken action when she'd seen the hapless Louise in Karl Reiner's toils. She hadn't hesitated—just marched straight up, got Louise out of the danger she was in. She'd cared enough about someone she hardly knew to risk making a scene, risk the anger of a powerful and influential man in her industry.

Madeline wouldn't have done that. Madeline would have laughed—found it amusing to see Louise's drink spiked. Or she would have simply shrugged and said the girl was an idiot. Rafael's eyes darkened. Or she'd have said she was smart—doing the right thing. Getting on the good side of a man who could help her career.

But she would no more have dreamt of intervening, of rescuing Louise, than she would have dreamt of caring a cent for the feelings of a man whose company she had bought out from under his nose, then trampled on his pride and kicked him scornfully into the dust.

Words sounded in his head. Celeste's voice…

'I am just like Madeline!'

His eyes blazed. Fists clenched suddenly. She was *nothing* like Madeline! He had hurled that at her and she'd refuted it, spewing out the sordid, unbearable reason for their alikeness…

His face contorted.

And is that it? Is that all she has to prove their similarity?

Memory of that hideous evening stabbed again—memory of him trying desperately to argue that she had been too young…that she'd been exploited and taken advantage of… that she must surely regret what she had done…

But she'd refuted that, too.

'No—I don't regret it.'

Her voice—so very clear, so very insistent.

His voice now, in his head, just as insistent.

It doesn't make sense!

The words forced themselves into his head, repeating themselves. *It doesn't make sense!*

Because it didn't. It couldn't. What Celeste had told him about what she had done—that she had just wanted quick, easy money and had no regrets about how she'd got it!— matched nothing else that he knew about her!

She'd turned down renewing her lucrative contract with Reiner Visage because she'd refused to give Karl Reiner what he wanted—sex in exchange for another year's contract! She'd refused to prostitute herself for her career—for easy money…

How did that match with what she had confessed to him?

Nothing he knew about her matched with her confession!

Memory blazed through him like a forest fire, igniting the undergrowth, ripping through his consciousness. Nothing in any memory of her until that last painful confession bore any indication at all that she could justify that insistence of hers! It was the one jarring note in everything he knew about her!

Making no sense at all.

He stilled. Like an unbearably slow gear wheel turning, his mind worked. The cogs of logic twisted, bringing up into his consciousness the one blazing truth that proved beyond all things just how much her insistence that she was like Madeline simply made no sense. How much it was a lie—*must* be a lie!

If she has no regrets for what she did, then why was she living a celibate life? Why had she cut herself off from all relationships with men? Why was she so obviously haunted and traumatised by her past? Why was it so painfully hard for her to come to trust me—to give herself to me—to accept me in her life?

He stood stock-still, feeling winded by the realisation. All around him people seemed to be moving like an inchoate sea, but he was alone in it. Slowly, clankingly, the wheels of logic turned again.

Madeline had no regrets—and she lived a life that showed it! A life that gave her her fill of affairs, of revelling in her sexual appetites!

Yet Celeste had withdrawn totally from that side of her existence. Shown extreme reluctance—every sign of trauma...

And that could mean only one thing—

She must regret what she did! She must! Or she would be as brazen as Madeline!

But why would she lie about it?

It can't be the truth—it can't! If she had no regrets, if she didn't care about what she'd done, then she would not have lived the lonely, passionless life she has...

Yet what reason could there be for lying about something that had destroyed everything they had together? Smashing to pieces all that was between them?

With infinite slowness the wheel inside his head made one last turn. If Celeste were not lying about regretting what she had done, even though what she had done had so clearly traumatised her, then there was only one other explanation for her insistence...

Only one.

Without conscious awareness he started to walk out of the crowded room. His hand slid inside his jacket pocket. Took out his mobile. He had calls to make. Urgent calls upon which his entire future happiness depended.

I have to be right about this! I have to be!

Desperation filled him. Mingled with the most precious quality in all the world. Hope—to which he clung with all his strength.

Celeste was packing. Not for another modelling assignment abroad, but to leave London. For good. She didn't know where she was going to go. She was just going. She'd let her flat, furnished, and tenants were moving in after the week-end. An agency would deal with them—deal with every-thing that came up. Her clothes and personal effects were locked away, and she'd cleaned the flat scrupulously. Now she just had to finish packing the case she was taking with her. Summer clothes, for somewhere warm, because she was cold to her very bones...

She wasn't going to stay in the UK—not even now that spring was finally approaching. She'd done the fashion weeks for this time of year and then had quit her agency.

Her last act had been to leave an encouraging card for Louise, to wish her luck in the career that was taking shape for her. Not that she needed any luck—she was doing well and, Celeste had been glad to see, was dating someone from outside the fashion world. Someone who was six foot two and played rugby—quite enough to take on the likes of Karl Reiner or similar, who might be intending to exploit Louise. Louise had wised up fast, and was pretty good at taking care of herself now.

She'd be OK from now on, Celeste knew.

And so will I—somehow!

How, she didn't know, because right now it was impossible to imagine being 'OK' by any definition of the word—unless it included 'functioning like an automaton'. But at least she *was* functioning, she thought. Functioning sufficiently to have done everything required to get to this point, where all she had to do was close her suitcase, pick up her handbag with her passport in it and head for the airport.

Where she would go precisely she wasn't yet sure. She might try Spain—it was cheap enough to live there prudently for a while, on her savings and the rental income from her flat, and it was warm. Then she frowned. No, of course she wouldn't go to Spain. She would hear Spanish spoken there, and that would remind her of Rafael...

There must be somewhere else. She ought to have thought about it earlier, but she hadn't wanted to. Thinking about it would have required planning, commitment, envisaging the future. And she couldn't do that. The future had stopped. Stopped when Rafael had turned his back on her and walked out through the door...

So where else is warm this time of year? Warm and not Spanish-speaking?

She made herself think, because thinking of somewhere warm to go at this time of year was better than thinking about Rafael turning his back on her and walking out of her life...

Where was it warm now? Where did people go to get away from the UK?

Dubai was popular—and very warm—everywhere in the Gulf was warm...

The guillotine slammed down in her head. She would be dead before she ever went to the Gulf again...

Frantically she thought of somewhere else. Where was it summer now?

Australia?

The guillotine slammed down again.

With a smothered cry, she seized up her bag. She would find somewhere warm to go when she got to the airport. Who cared where? She didn't. She would never care about anything again.

Or anyone...

Pain clamped around her heart, but she ignored it. She always ignored it. There was nothing else to do but ignore it. And keep functioning. That was important.

And finding somewhere warm, even though her bones were cold...so very cold...

The entry bell to the house sounded. Her taxi had arrived. She picked up her suitcase. Her keys. The agent already had keys to give to the tenants. She looked around her bedroom one last time but could feel nothing. She was too cold to feel anything. Carrying her suitcase, she went into her little hallway and buzzed open the front door, to show the taxi driver she knew he was there. Then she put on her coat, busying herself doing it up because it would be chilly outside. Then she opened her flat door, casting one last look around, in case there was something she had missed.

But there was nothing. Nothing left of her.

Nothing left of her anywhere.

She stepped out onto the landing, moving to pull her flat door shut behind her.

And stopped dead.

Rafael was coming up the last flight of stairs towards her.

She couldn't move. Could not move a muscle. This wasn't real. This wasn't happening. It could not be happening...

Yet there he was, striding across the short outer landing

right up to her door, right up to *her.* She opened her mouth to protest. To protest that this could not be happening, that it was impossible. That he'd walked out of her flat long, nightmare months ago and could never return...

He took her shoulders and she saw by the sweep of his eyes that he'd seen her suitcase. A flashing frown showed on his brow, but he simply manoeuvred her back inside her hallway, picking up the suitcase as though it was a feather and depositing it inside, then turned to shut the flat door.

'I want to talk to you—'

His voice was deep, harsh. His eyes burned as they ground into hers.

She felt faint, dizzy. Heard him saying more.

'I *have* to talk to you!'

There was still harshness in his voice, but there was more, too—a powerful, urgent emotion that impelled him forward so that she had to step backwards, back into her living room. She took another stumbling step away from his grip, which was burning through the layer of her coat to the skin beneath.

His rapid, sweeping glance was traversing the room, seeing its bareness—there was nothing of her there any more, no books or ornaments, only furniture and curtains. The flashing frown came again, and his eyes returned to her.

'Where are you going?' he demanded. 'The empty flat, the suitcase...'

She found her voice. Finally forced her strangled throat to open.

'I'm leaving,' she said. 'I've rented out my flat and I'm going abroad.'

Emotion knifed through him. She had so nearly disappeared again!

I got here just in time.

'Where?' he heard his voice demanding.

'I don't know...' She spoke almost randomly, unable to force her mind into coherent thought. Because her mind was not working at all. It had been overwhelmed by emotion. Emotion that was pouring through her like scalding water.

I can't bear to see him again—I can't bear it!

To see him here again, in the flesh, in physical reality instead of just in the dreams that had tormented her, slain her, all these long months since he had gone, was unbearable.

'Well,' he said, and there was something different in his voice now, beneath the harshness that was still in it, 'how about Australia? After all...' and now his eyes had changed, too '...you have dual UK-Australian citizenship—'

She paled. 'How...how do you know?'

But that wasn't really the question she was asking.

Why did he know?

His eyes pinioned hers, as dark, as heavy as basalt. 'I know a lot about you, Celeste. A lot more than I did. Which is why...' he took a heavy, searing breath '...why I have to talk to you.'

She was shaking her head. 'No,' she said. *'No.'*

His hands came onto her shoulders again. 'Yes, Celeste,' he said. His voice was different again, and something in it made her throat constrict.

'Sit down,' he said.

He pressed her shoulders, not roughly but insistently, and her knees buckled. With a jerk she sat down on the sofa, indenting the cushions she'd lined up so neatly, ready for her tenant to find a pristine flat. He sat down heavily at the far end. There was empty space between them. Yet it seemed to her that there was a force field emanating from him that was holding her in a traction she could not escape. She had to try—

'I've got to go,' she said. 'I've got a taxi coming.'

Even as she spoke the entry phone went again. She tried to rise, but Rafael was before her. He strode out to her hallway and she heard him press the intercom, heard him dismiss the taxi, then stride back in again. He stood there a moment, looking down at her. So tall, so overpowering...

She couldn't breathe, but she had to. Had to go on breathing in and breathing out, even though her mind had left her body. She could not think or speak—could do nothing except sit there, like a bag of nerveless bones, on her sofa.

Slowly, deliberately, he sat himself back down. He looked at her as she sat, clutching her handbag as if it were a breathing aid.

'You're too thin,' he said abruptly, his eyes sweeping over her critically. 'Far too thin.'

She said nothing. What did it matter what she looked like? What did anything matter at all? What could it matter ever again?

He was speaking to her and she had to hear him—had to let the words reach her ears though she tried to block them. But it was impossible. They penetrated every last desperate layer of her defence.

His voice was sombre, carrying a weight in it that seemed to bow and bend his words.

'It took me a long, long time to realise something, Celeste. But eventually it dawned on me—I realised what it was that was wrong about what you said to me. You said…' he spoke with incised deliberation '…that you did not regret what you did when you were seventeen, that you had no regrets even now, as an adult.'

He took a breath. It was time to say what he had flown here to say. Time to stake all his future happiness, his very reason for being, on what he said next.

'There are only two reasons why someone would say that.' His eyes were on her, like a beam of laser light she could not escape. 'Either it's because, like Madeline, they're perfectly happy with their behaviour—see nothing wrong in it, nothing to object to, no big deal.' He paused. 'Or one other reason.'

His eyes shifted a moment, gazing out into nowhere, then came back to her. 'Tell me…how do you happen to have dual citizenship?'

She didn't answer, but she didn't need to.

'Your father was Australian,' Rafael said. 'You were born there. But your mother was English, and when your father died you came back to the UK, grew up here. When you were seventeen you went back again, and stayed there for several years, only returning when you were twenty.' He paused again—a longer pause. His eyes never left her.

She sat numb, her face drained of colour. Remorselessly he went on.

'It's an expensive journey, from the UK to Australia. And you were raised in a council flat, weren't you? So there wasn't any spare money around. Certainly not enough to fund not only getting to Australia but the lavish lifestyle you enjoyed there. Because you lived it up royally there, didn't you, Celeste? First-class hotels and resorts, travelling right across the continent, from Perth to the Great Barrier Reef. It must have cost thousands. Thousands upon thousands! Especially,' he finished, 'when there were two of you to pay for...'

Her hands were clenched on her bag, her knuckles white. She knew what was coming next—knew he must have discovered everything, since he had found out so much already.

He spoke gently. Quietly. And so, so carefully.

'I've seen her death certificate, Celeste. My researchers in Australia obtained an official copy and sent it to me. I've brought it with me.' He reached inside his jacket, took out a folded document, unfolded it slowly.

'I don't want to see it!' Her voice was high-pitched.

'And I have your father's, too,' he said, his eyes never leaving hers. But they were gentle now, like his voice. 'They were both signed at the same registrar's office in New South Wales—fifteen years apart.'

He paused again.

'You told me about your father, Celeste. You told me that he'd drowned in a rough sea. But you did *not* say that he drowned while he was rescuing another surfer who had got into difficulties. I've seen the newspaper clippings from when it happened—he was given a posthumous award. There's a photo of your mother receiving it on his behalf. You're holding her hand—you were two years old.'

'I've seen it!' she cried, her voice anguished. 'I've seen it so many times. My mother treasured it! And I can't bear to see it again! She cried every time she looked at it. Every time! She loved him so much!'

She felt her hand being taken. Loosened from her clenched grip on her bag.

'Loved him so much,' echoed Rafael, in that same gentle voice that was a torment to hear, 'that she wanted to go back to Australia to die in the same place he had.'

His eyes went to the death certificate for Celeste's mother. Forty-two years old. No age to die. His eyes shadowed. But then cancer found its victims at every stage of their lives. His eyes lifted to Celeste. There were tears in her eyes now.

Gently he squeezed her hand, and she could feel his warmth, his strength running into her. Giving her the strength to speak at last.

After so many years.

'She was diagnosed when she was already terminal,' she said. 'Ovarian cancer is like that—the silent killer, it's called, because its symptoms are so hard to spot. Especially if, like Mum, you ignore them.' She swallowed. 'It's the reason I have routine ultrasound scans every year—to spot it early if it starts in me, too. Mum made me promise—she dreaded the same thing happening to me as had to her.'

Her voice was low and halting, but she went on. Forcing herself to speak. To relive the fear and the anguish and the grief and the loss. 'She left Australia straight after my father's funeral. She couldn't bear to be there any more, without him. But after she was diagnosed, and knew she could not survive, she wanted to go back—to die in the place he'd loved so much that had killed him in the end. And she wanted to do what they'd done for their honeymoon—backpack all around Australia, seeing everything, thinking they had all the time in the world to live together for all the years to come. But all they got was a bare three years.'

'So you took her back there, didn't you?' said Rafael quietly. 'You took her back and went with her all around the country, retracing the journey she'd taken with your father. And then you went to the surf spot he loved so much, when she got weaker and weaker, and she died there. And you buried her next to him. And they lie there together, Celeste—side by side, at the sea's edge.'

She was weeping now, the tears running silently down her cheeks. He brushed them with his fingers and her face buckled more.

'It was to pay for all of that that you did what you did. That you became a summer bride.'

She was silent. She could not speak.

'You said…' He spoke carefully, for this was very, very important. 'You said that you did it because you wanted money fast. But what you did not say was why.'

She looked at him. 'What difference does it make?' she said, and her eyes had that deadened expression in them now. 'You asked if I regretted doing it—and I don't. I made the decision I needed to make, and I would do the same again. And I have no remorse, or regret—not a single shred! If I could have done it differently, I would have. But this was the only way.'

He dropped her hand. Got to his feet in a jerking movement. Stared down at her.

'What difference does it make?' he echoed. 'How can you even think that, let alone believe it?' His eyes flashed. 'It makes all the difference in the world!'

'No, it *doesn't!*' Her own eyes flashed now, with hatred—hatred for herself and what she had done, for what she would do again without the slightest hesitation or remorse or regret. 'I still did it! I still sold myself for sex! A summer bride. I was driven out to some villa at the edge of the city and I went through a travesty of a ceremony, in a language I didn't understand and didn't need to, because all that was required of me was that I did what I had been paid to do—*paid to do!*'

She took a ragged, ravaging breath.

'And to ensure I was docile and submissive I was given something to drink every night—something like roofies, I suppose. It turned everything into a kind of fog and I was so, so grateful. Because it blurred everything...everything that was going on...everything that was done to me...'

Her voice changed, he could hear it, and her gaze now followed the long, dark tunnel leading back into her past.

'Sometimes,' she said, 'I had to wait. In a courtyard, on a terrace or a rooftop. I don't remember too well.' Her face furrowed. 'I just remember that it was cold, and I was given some kind of wrap. And I used to look up and see stars. Stars that were very far away. I liked that. I liked that they were so far away...so far away from everything that I was doing...'

She stopped, and yet again her voice changed, becoming a kind of harsh whisper.

'I wanted to be part of the heavens. I wanted to be taken up there—away from everything down here on the earth, away from everything that was happening to me. I wanted to be amongst the stars—as far away as they were. Because I could not *bear* what was happening.'

She swallowed. 'Except it *was* happening...and I had to let it happen...or else my mother would die without seeing again the one place in the world where she had been happy, without getting to the one place in the world where she wanted to die—'

She stopped again, and this time she did not continue.

Rafael reached his hands down to her, taking both of hers so that her handbag fell to the floor, unregarded. He drew her up, still holding her hands.

'I want you to understand something,' he said. 'Something that is very, very important for you to understand.' He spoke carefully, because what he said now was the most important thing he would say in all his life. 'We are judged,

Celeste, not only by our acts, but by our reasons for those acts. It is the deed *and* the intent for that deed. Do you understand me? Do you understand?'

His voice was shaking with the immensity of what he had to get across, what he *had* to make her comprehend, even though she was looking at him with a deadened blankness in her eyes that was like a knife in his body.

'It is because you did what you did not for yourself but for your dying mother that it is entirely and totally different! You forced yourself to do something that repelled you so much it traumatised you for years! It shut you in a prison of celibacy, cut you off from all normal relationships! That isn't the reaction of someone who has no regrets because they don't consider they did anything they didn't *want* to do!'

He took a ragged breath, clasped his hands around the cusps of her shoulders. 'To think that you stood here and compared yourself to Madeline! Insisted you were exactly the same! God Almighty—if you had only *told* me that night what you've told me now—what I had to find out for myself once my imbecilic brain had finally worked out what the *hell* was going on in your head! What had gone on in your life. Because if you had…'

His voice changed. Now it had a timbre in it that found its way into her nerveless body as she stood like a limp rag, scarcely able to keep standing without his hold on her.

'If you had, then I would have done what I will do now, my most precious Celeste,' he said.

And now his eyes were changing, too. The blaze of anger in them—anger at her silence, at his own unforgivable stupidity and blindness—was gone now, and in its place was not a fire, but a glow…a glow as warm as the palms of his hands curved over her shoulders.

'I would have begged your forgiveness for not trusting you, not trusting everything I knew about you, not trusting everything we had together. I would have begged you, implored you, to come back to me.'

His eyes poured down into hers, reaching to her heart.

'I would have begged you, implored you,' he said softly, 'to love me as I love you, as I always will love you, for your heart alone.'

He kissed her softly and cherishingly.

She looked up at him, not daring to believe. 'I saw the revulsion in your eyes.' Her voice was low, and shaken. 'I saw it when you told me about Madeline. When I told you about myself.'

He looked down at her. 'Do you see it now?' he asked. 'Do you see *anything* but love, Celeste?' He shook his head. 'You will never see it. Never see anything but love for all our days. What you did,' he said, 'took courage I doubt many could find, and I have for you, my most precious Celeste, only the deepest respect. I told you once, when I was condemning Madeline, that I would never condemn any woman who was driven into prostitution by desperation. Do you think you were different? Do you think you did it for any other reason than to give to your mother her dying wish?' His gaze poured into hers. 'What you did, you did as an act of love,' he said.

He did not wait for her to answer. Waited only to see the darkness in her eyes finally start to clear. Letting back in the light of life. Of love.

Then, and only then, did he sweep her into his arms and hold her close, so very close, against his heart. Where he would keep her for ever.

She was weeping now, he could tell. Her thin body shuddered as he wrapped her against him. He let her weep, holding her safe in his arms. And when she was done and she lifted her head, her cheeks stained with tears, her eyes clinging to his just as her body clung to his, he looked down at her.

'Shall we go now?' he said, his voice still soft, still cherishing. 'Shall we go together, as we shall be from now on—where we belong, with each other?'

He smoothed her hair, kissed her again, then loosed his arms and simply took her hand. He bent to pick up her handbag and gave it to her. Then he walked with her to the door and picked up her suitcase.

She looked at him, her heart beating…soaring… Soaring like a bird towards the heavens… Leaving the past behind—for ever, this time…

'Where?' she breathed.

Her eyes were wide—wide with hoping, with finally daring to believe. To believe everything he was telling her.

'Into our future,' he told her.

EPILOGUE

THE WARM BREEZE lifted the fine netting of her veil. Through its misted folds Celeste could see the brilliant sunlit cobalt-blue of the Pacific. Feel the warmth of the sunshine on her face as she gazed towards the gazebo at the end of the pathway. Its position was perfect, framed by white bougainvillaea, enclosed in a little private glade from the rest of the gardens, and with the vista of the ocean behind it.

But it was not the gazebo that held her gaze. It was the man waiting for her.

Rafael—her beloved Rafael! Who had freed her with his love—freed her to love him as he, as she knew from every loving glance he gave her, loved her.

Her heart constricted. How much she loved him! How very, very much! He was looking back to her now, his dark eyes smiling with all the love in them that she had in hers for him. The priest was waiting for her and she started to walk forward, as tall and graceful as a lily in her wedding gown. Soft Hawaiian music played from hidden speakers and the scent of exotic blooms wafted to her.

She reached Rafael's side and stood beside him, her heart singing with happiness. They had eyes only for each other. When the service began she gave her responses clear and low, as his were clear and resonant. She could feel her heart swell.

Then, at last, as the priest raised his hand in blessing of them both, Rafael's mouth dipped to hers.

'Señora Sanguardo...' he whispered to her.

'For ever,' she whispered back.

Then, hand in hand, they walked back with the priest to the wedding breakfast that awaited them. And to the rest of their life together.

* * * * *

ROMANCE

The Only Woman to Defy Him	Carol Marinelli
Secrets of a Ruthless Tycoon	Cathy Williams
Gambling with the Crown	Lynn Raye Harris
The Forbidden Touch of Sanguardo	Julia James
One Night to Risk it All	Maisey Yates
A Clash with Cannavaro	Elizabeth Power
The Truth About De Campo	Jennifer Hayward
Sheikh's Scandal	Lucy Monroe
Beach Bar Baby	Heidi Rice
Sex, Lies & Her Impossible Boss	Jennifer Rae
Lessons in Rule-Breaking	Christy McKellen
Twelve Hours of Temptation	Shoma Narayanan
Expecting the Prince's Baby	Rebecca Winters
The Millionaire's Homecoming	Cara Colter
The Heir of the Castle	Scarlet Wilson
Swept Away by the Tycoon	Barbara Wallace
Return of Dr Maguire	Judy Campbell
Heatherdale's Shy Nurse	Abigail Gordon

MEDICAL

200 Harley Street: The Proud Italian	Alison Roberts
200 Harley Street: American Surgeon in London	Lynne Marshall
A Mother's Secret	Scarlet Wilson
Saving His Little Miracle	Jennifer Taylor

0414GEN STD HB

Mills & Boon® Large Print
May 2014

ROMANCE

The Dimitrakos Proposition	Lynne Graham
His Temporary Mistress	Cathy Williams
A Man Without Mercy	Miranda Lee
The Flaw in His Diamond	Susan Stephens
Forged in the Desert Heat	Maisey Yates
The Tycoon's Delicious Distraction	Maggie Cox
A Deal with Benefits	Susanna Carr
Mr (Not Quite) Perfect	Jessica Hart
English Girl in New York	Scarlet Wilson
The Greek's Tiny Miracle	Rebecca Winters
The Final Falcon Says I Do	Lucy Gordon

HISTORICAL

From Ruin to Riches	Louise Allen
Protected by the Major	Anne Herries
Secrets of a Gentleman Escort	Bronwyn Scott
Unveiling Lady Clare	Carol Townend
A Marriage of Notoriety	Diane Gaston

MEDICAL

Gold Coast Angels: Bundle of Trouble	Fiona Lowe
Gold Coast Angels: How to Resist Temptation	Amy Andrews
Her Firefighter Under the Mistletoe	Scarlet Wilson
Snowbound with Dr Delectable	Susan Carlisle
Her Real Family Christmas	Kate Hardy
Christmas Eve Delivery	Connie Cox

0414 GEN STD LP

ROMANCE

Ravelli's Defiant Bride	Lynne Graham
When Da Silva Breaks the Rules	Abby Green
The Heartbreaker Prince	Kim Lawrence
The Man She Can't Forget	Maggie Cox
A Question of Honour	Kate Walker
What the Greek Can't Resist	Maya Blake
An Heir to Bind Them	Dani Collins
Playboy's Lesson	Melanie Milburne
Don't Tell the Wedding Planner	Aimee Carson
The Best Man for the Job	Lucy King
Falling for Her Rival	Jackie Braun
More than a Fling?	Joss Wood
Becoming the Prince's Wife	Rebecca Winters
Nine Months to Change His Life	Marion Lennox
Taming Her Italian Boss	Fiona Harper
Summer with the Millionaire	Jessica Gilmore
Back in Her Husband's Arms	Susanne Hampton
Wedding at Sunday Creek	Leah Martyn

MEDICAL

200 Harley Street: The Soldier Prince	Kate Hardy
200 Harley Street: The Enigmatic Surgeon	Annie Claydon
A Father for Her Baby	Sue MacKay
The Midwife's Son	Sue MacKay

Mills & Boon® Large Print

June 2014

ROMANCE

A Bargain with the Enemy	Carole Mortimer
A Secret Until Now	Kim Lawrence
Shamed in the Sands	Sharon Kendrick
Seduction Never Lies	Sara Craven
When Falcone's World Stops Turning	Abby Green
Securing the Greek's Legacy	Julia James
An Exquisite Challenge	Jennifer Hayward
Trouble on Her Doorstep	Nina Harrington
Heiress on the Run	Sophie Pembroke
The Summer They Never Forgot	Kandy Shepherd
Daring to Trust the Boss	Susan Meier

HISTORICAL

Portrait of a Scandal	Annie Burrows
Drawn to Lord Ravenscar	Anne Herries
Lady Beneath the Veil	Sarah Mallory
To Tempt a Viking	Michelle Willingham
Mistress Masquerade	Juliet Landon

MEDICAL

From Venice with Love	Alison Roberts
Christmas with Her Ex	Fiona McArthur
After the Christmas Party...	Janice Lynn
Her Mistletoe Wish	Lucy Clark
Date with a Surgeon Prince	Meredith Webber
Once Upon a Christmas Night...	Annie Claydon

0514 GEN STD LP